The Captain's Lady

Terri Kennedy

ISBN-13: 978-0-9975032-1-0

Parker River Press
PO Box 242
South Yarmouth, MA 02664

www.TerriKennedy.com/ParkerRiverPress

To Howard
Thank you for all your encouragement and support.

ONE

Captain Richard Mortimer noticed her as soon as she entered the taproom. She skulked past the other diners to the table in the far corner, slouching slightly as she went, using her cloak as a shield to conceal her face. Her attempt to make herself invisible failed. Every male eye in the room followed her. Her clothes gave her away, of course. The quality was much too fine to mistake her for a local farm girl or a middle-class matron en route to visit a friend. She was clearly a young woman of gentle birth and not some strumpet soliciting business for the night. He waited to see who would join her, a husband perhaps or father. Maybe only a servant or companion.

The night had turned foul—a violent rainstorm had turned the roads into mud too deep for the heavy coaches to traverse. Even his hired carriage, though much lighter, had become mired several times before he and his batman, Nelson, had decided to waylay for the night and finish their journey in the morning. Hers was but the latest coach to find refuge at the inn.

Within a few minutes it became apparent she was alone.

He realized it only moments before every other man in the crowded room did. It didn't take long for one brave fellow, emboldened by drink, to make his way over to her.

Mortimer groaned.

He did not want to relinquish his coveted seat by the fire. But he knew he'd have to. Even if the quality of her clothing hadn't declared that she was no light-skirt ready to do business, her demeanor did. She looked terrified.

He couldn't hear what the fellow said to her, but he could see she didn't appreciate it. She shook her head and shrank back in her chair as though trying to fade into the wall behind her.

Damn.

Mortimer downed the last gulp of his ale. Reluctantly, he took hold of the cane he'd left resting on the chair next to him, the chair he was saving for Nelson upon his return from settling the carriage driver and his horses in the stable. Slowly, he rose from his warm, cherished, hearth-side seat. Leaning heavily on the cane, he made his way over to the other side of the room.

"Come on, now, love, just a quick tumble. I'll leave you satisfied, I will."

"Sir, if you do not apologize to my wife this instant, I shall be compelled to call you out."

From his seated position, the man eyed him warily, no doubt noting the light blue jacket that declared Mortimer a member of the Light Dragoons.

"Your wife, you say? Sorry, Cap'n, didn't know. Apologies, ma'am." He quickly made his exit, vacating the seat across from the lady.

Mortimer sank down in it gratefully. He shifted uncomfortably, trying to ease the throbbing in his thigh where the lead ball remained lodged despite all the physicians' best efforts.

"Forgive me, madam, for my impertinence, but it seemed the most expedient way to remove your suitor without my having to actually manhandle him."

She looked no more at ease with him sitting across from her than she had the drunkard.

"Allow me to introduce myself. I am Captain Richard Mortimer, lately of the Peninsula. If I have overstepped, I shall leave, but it appeared to me you did not welcome that man's attentions. I thought only to relieve you of them."

"Can I get you anything, Miss? Another ale, Captain?" The serving girl appeared by their table.

"Have you eaten?" Mortimer asked the lady, but she didn't reply, keeping her eyes downcast. "We'll have a meat pie, a tankard of ale for me, and tea for the lady, please Becky."

As soon as Becky moved out of earshot, his taciturn companion finally spoke.

"I can't pay for the food," she said, obviously embarrassed by this lack of funds.

"Please, allow me."

"Why?" She didn't trust him, and why should she?

"Because you need it. Now, why don't you tell me what you are doing here all alone."

"I'm on my way to Bath to visit my aunt. The coach couldn't continue so we have to put up here for the night. It's an unexpected stop. Had we made it all the way to Bath today as planned, my aunt would have met me."

"Where is your maid?"

She looked around the room guiltily.

"She became ill and got off at the last stop."

He didn't believe her. She was, perhaps, planning an assignation with a lover but the unplanned stopover delayed her. Her lover, no doubt, awaited her arrival in Bath.

She seemed incredibly young and Mortimer felt extremely old. He'd seen too many girls used and left behind on the Peninsula. Whatever scoundrel had convinced her to run away with him deserved to be shot.

"What is your name?" He used his captain's voice, the one that brooked no argument. Many a raw recruit had crumpled at the sound of that voice. She was not immune to its effects.

"Jenny Carlisle."

"Well, Miss Carlisle, I assume it is Miss Carlisle?"

She nodded.

"Well, Miss Carlisle, you've gotten yourself into quite a predicament here." He could see her acknowledgement in her eyes. She knew she'd made a mistake setting out on her own as she had. Taking charge as he was accustomed to doing, he beckoned Becky over.

"I need a room for Miss Carlisle," he ordered.

"I'm sorry, Captain, we're full up. All the rooms have already been taken. Best I can do is offer to share my straw bed in the attic, but she'll have to wait until I'm done down here."

"How much is it?" Jenny asked before Mortimer could continue.

"Only two shillings, Miss."

Jenny shook her head, and Becky left to wait on a raucous group of local boys.

"You will take my room. My man, Nelson, and I will bed down in the stables with our horses. It is not the worst sleeping accommodations we've ever had."

"I couldn't possibly take your room, sir. If you do want to help, you could please lend me two shillings so I can join Becky in the attic. You must give me your direction so I can repay you as soon as I get to my aunt's."

"Have you ever slept in an attic, Miss Carlisle? It's cold

and drafty. Straw beds have fleas. I will not allow you to endure such conditions."

He didn't know what he'd said, but it transformed her from a meek, timid, frightened little girl to a virago.

"You are in no position to allow or disallow anything, sir. Despite what you claimed to that ruffian, you are not my husband, not my father, not even my friend. You are a stranger whom I have no more reason to trust than any other man in this room. I do not answer to you."

Mortimer smiled. The girl had backbone. Though misguided, she at least showed some fortitude.

"My apologies. Please, allow me to offer you my room. You would be doing me a service, you see, because I would not be able to rest worrying about you." She was going to turn him down, he knew. Mortimer felt intense weariness. "Miss Carlisle, I have just returned from the Peninsula. I have seen all manner of horrors. I have seen what men do to unprotected women." That drew a startled look from her. "Please, allow me this small gesture. For your protection, for my peace of mind. Take my room and sleep."

Thankfully, Becky arrived with their order before Jenny had to answer. She could have told Captain Mortimer a thing or two about the dangers unprotected women faced, but she restrained herself.

The food smelled wonderful. Jenny couldn't help herself—her mouth watered at the sight of the meat pie. She hadn't eaten a thing all day, had barely eaten anything at dinner the previous night. She was starving. Still, she hesitated, uncomfortable accepting the captain's charity.

Captain Mortimer seemed to know what she was thinking. He picked up the fork and cut off a mouthful. Waving the fork in front of her face, he said, "Eat."

She opened her mouth, and he fed her the best tasting bite she'd ever had. He handed her the fork. No use pretending any longer. She dove into the meat pie with gusto.

Captain Mortimer leaned back in his chair and sipped his ale while she ate every last bite.

"Now that you are fed," he said as she licked the last bit of juice from the fork, "you should get yourself upstairs to bed."

"I can't take your room. You're wounded. I don't mind sleeping in the attic, honestly I don't. I won't be able to sleep thinking about you out in the cold stable."

"We appear to be at an impasse," he said thoughtfully.

Just then a whoop of laughter came from the table of local boys as Becky dragged one of the young men out of his seat.

"Sorry, Miss, I won't be able to offer you that bed in the attic after all," Becky said as she went by with her young man in tow.

"Well," Mortimer said. "Now that's settled." He laboriously got to his feet. Jenny had to keep herself from assisting him. Somehow, she didn't think he would appreciate her offering a helping hand. Standing beside her chair leaning on his cane, he held his elbow out to her. "Miss Carlisle?"

She could be obstinate, she knew. She could refuse to take his arm and remain right here in the taproom. And be accosted by unwanted male attention all night. She was taking a risk trusting him, she knew that too. But there was something about him, a world-weariness that made her feel safe in his company. She hadn't felt safe in weeks.

"Very well, Captain," she said, rising and placing her hand on his elbow. "I shall accept your kind offer and make use of your room tonight."

"Thank you, Miss Carlisle. I ask only that you vacate it first thing so I may make use of it to freshen up before I continue my journey."

He walked her to the foot of the stairs, then gave her the key.

"My things are already in there. Make use of whatever you need." He bent briefly over her hand. "May I have the pleasure of your company at breakfast?"

"Captain Mortimer, you are the most chivalrous gentleman it has ever been my good fortune to meet." She squeezed his hand and felt tears form in her eyes. "Thank you, sir. I think you are my guardian angel tonight, just when I had lost faith in all that is holy."

She ran up the stairs, leaving him standing at the bottom staring after her.

∞∞∞∞

"What're you doing out here?" Nelson asked when Mortimer joined him in the stable.

Mortimer sat down heavily on a bale of straw, joining the circle of grooms and hostlers who Nelson regaled with tales of his peninsula adventures. In exchange for the entertaining stories, the workmen shared the contents of their flasks. Though Nelson could drink just about any man under the table, Mortimer could see he was well lit.

A flask landed in Mortimer's hand and he drank heartily and thankfully before passing it on. His leg burned. He yearned to find his bed, the very one he had just given away.

"Forgive me, Nelson, but the soft bed I promised you tonight is gone. I gave it away."

Nelson shrugged. "One more night of sleeping on the cold ground makes no difference one way or a'tother. Who did you give our bed to?"

"A damsel in distress."

"Well, then, you had no choice, did you?" Nelson went over to the bags he had retrieved from their carriage and got out his own flask. He handed it to Mortimer, then went about making a comfortable place for them to sleep in an empty stall. "Won't do that leg of yours much good, though, will it? Next time you rescue a damsel in distress, perhaps you should try joining her in the bed."

"We both know she'd be in no danger from me if I did," Mortimer said quietly so only Nelson could hear.

"How'd you get wounded, Captain?" a young hostler asked.

Mortimer sighed. Young men loved war stories. Lord knew, he'd grown up on them. He had been so excited at the prospect of battle. But he'd had too many years of battles and now just wanted to go home.

"Nothing dramatic, I'm afraid," Mortimer obliged the young man. "A rifleman shot me off my horse in the Portugal hills."

"On your way to deliver an important message to General Howard," Nelson elaborated. "The shooter kept us pinned down for nearly two days. No one could get to Captain Mortimer because he'd fallen down a ravine. He ordered us to keep going, to get the message to the General. Half the company pressed on, but the rest of us held our ground until we could rescue the captain. Thought we'd be bringing in a corpse, we did, but stubborn cuss that he is, he managed to survive."

"And I should have had you all court-martialed for disobeying a direct order." Mortimer limped over to the straw pallet Nelson had prepared and settled himself down. A soft feather bed was highly overrated, he was sure.

It would feel all the more wonderful tomorrow night when he finally lay his head once again in his own home. Fairleigh.

When he'd left ten years ago, he never expected to see it again. He certainly never expected to come back as its master.

He'd bought his commission at eighteen, eager to be off on his own, away from the oppressive tyranny of his father. Army life had suited Mortimer, he felt more at home in a barracks than he'd ever felt as a child in his own home.

He hadn't returned for his father's funeral six years ago. In truth, it had been long over before word reached him his father had died. No point returning after that. He and his father would never make peace.

His older brother, Elliot, inherited Fairleigh and all their father's other property. He and Elliot were only two years apart in age but had never been allowed to be brothers. Elliot was the heir, Richard only the spare.

Sadly, two years ago, the spare had become necessary. Elliot died of influenza before dutifully marrying and producing an heir.

Mortimer should have returned then, but he didn't want to. He had never wanted Fairleigh, had never envied Elliot his inheritance. If he hadn't been wounded, he would be on the Peninsula still, doing what he was trained to do. What suited him.

Tomorrow, he would return home to see his mother and the younger sister he barely knew. She'd been a child of seven when he'd left, and he hadn't seen her since.

Mortimer leaned back in the straw bed and fell into a dreamless sleep.

∞∞∞∞∞

Jenny locked the door and put a chair under the latch to keep anyone from forcing his way in. Captain Mortimer had seemed kind, but she'd been fooled before. She secured the window then turned down the covers on the bed. It looked soft and inviting.

Jenny had only a small bag with her into which she'd thrown a hodgepodge of items. Her decision to run had been sudden and unexpected. Until moments before she'd snuck out of her father's house, she'd been convinced there was no escape, no alternative to the fate that awaited her.

But when her maid, Dolly, had knocked on her door and told her it was time to get dressed, she knew she couldn't go through with it.

So, she'd run.

She went through the bag now. She had a nightgown and a hairbrush. Her journal. The locket her Aunt Julia had given her when she turned sixteen. A dozen hairpins. One stocking.

She took off her still damp cloak and hung it over the chair. She pulled her dress over her head, the only dress she owned that she could get on and off without the assistance of her lady's maid and the only dress she'd brought with her.

She kicked off her shoes and removed her stockings. She'd have to make them last as she had no other pair.

It would be humorous if it weren't so tragic. What had she done?

She knew Aunt Julia would welcome her. She hoped her aunt would understand and help her stand up to her father.

Jenny took the pins from her hair. She put them in the box with the others she'd brought. Picking up her brush, she brushed her nearly black hair to a bluish sheen, then corded it into a single, waist-length braid for sleeping.

Putting on her nightgown, she crawled into bed.

She thought she would have trouble sleeping, but the day's events had so exhausted her she fell instantly to sleep. With her last conscious thought she wondered how Captain Mortimer slept.

∞∞∞∞

Morning dawned clear and bright. The sun poured right into Jenny's eyes. She stretched and rolled over, momentarily forgetting where she was and what she was about. A knock on the door brought her instantly back.

"Captain Mortimer would like you to join him belowstairs, ma'am," Becky called from outside the door.

Jenny flew about the room, dressing and packing as quickly as she could. She grabbed her cloak and her bag and headed downstairs. Becky showed her to a private parlor. After being so crowded last night, the inn seemed surprisingly empty this morning.

"Good morning, did you sleep well?" Captain Mortimer greeted her when she entered the room. He started to rise, but Jenny noticed his wince of pain and motioned him to remain seated. He didn't object and appeared relieved to dispense with the social niceties for the moment. As for herself, Jenny felt guilty enough about taking his bed without adding to his discomfort by making him stand. Social niceties were not the true mark of a gentleman anyway, she'd learned through hard experience.

"Wonderfully," she replied, seating herself at the table, which held a spread of toast, eggs, and sausage. "I can't thank you enough, Captain. I will repay you for your kindness, I promise you." She piled a hefty portion from the platters onto his plate and set it before him, then prepared a similar plate for herself.

After the past few weeks when she could barely keep anything down and hardly ate at all, it seemed her appetite had returned with a vengeance. Her stomach rumbled in anticipation as she inhaled the enticing scent of sausage.

"Will your aunt be meeting the coach in Bath?" he asked, and Jenny's appetite nearly deserted her again.

She hesitated, then answered truthfully.

"She doesn't know when to expect me." In fact, Aunt Julia wasn't expecting her at all—she had no idea Jenny was coming.

Jenny nibbled on a piece of toast.

"This breakfast is delicious. Now I owe you for two meals as well as that comfortable bed you shared with me last night."

Captain Mortimer smiled, and Jenny's face heated as she realized what she'd said. "That is, the bed you let me sleep in," she stammered. "By myself."

Blast the man, he could say something to ease her gaffe, but he merely bit off a piece of sausage and chewed. Slowly. Jenny found she couldn't take her eyes off his lips and the way they puckered and smoothed as he chewed, his mustache twitching as his jaw moved.

She pulled her gaze away and attended to her own meal.

"Please, sir, you must give me your direction so that I can send remuneration when I get to Bath."

"No remuneration is necessary, Miss Carlisle, I assure you. Still. . ." He handed her a slip of paper. "I have no cards yet," he said in explanation.

Jenny glanced at the paper he'd given her and saw that he'd written, in a fine, sure hand the location of his estate.

"May I have your card, Miss Carlisle?"

Jenny reached for her reticule then caught herself. As kind as Captain Mortimer had been, and as handsome as she found him, she still wasn't sure she wanted to see him again. She couldn't bear to see his disappointment, or more likely, his disgust, when he learned the truth about her.

"I don't know exactly where I'll be staying in Bath," she lied and immediately regretted it. Fortunately, he let the matter drop. Perhaps he had asked out of courtesy and had no desire to see her again, either. It surprised her how disappointed she felt at the thought.

His man Nelson came in then, and Captain Mortimer made the introductions.

"We'd best be getting underway, Captain," Nelson reminded him.

Captain Mortimer bowed to her on his way out. "Please remain in the parlor until your coach is ready to leave, Miss Carlisle. Have a safe trip."

When he left, Jenny felt more alone than she had the day before. She wanted to run after him and give him her direction, almost beg him to call on her at her aunt's house. But she didn't. Captain Mortimer gave every appearance of being a good, kind, decent man. He deserved a woman better than she.

The driver called the passengers to board the coach. Jenny gathered her things and left the private parlor. She had almost made it to the outside door when someone grabbed her arm and spun her around.

"Going somewhere?".

TWO

Jenny froze. She couldn't believe he had followed her, couldn't believe how easily he had found her.

"You embarrassed me in front of all London Society yesterday, Jenny my love. For that you will pay." He squeezed her arm so hard she could almost feel the bruise forming.

"Miss Carlisle, you left your hairbrush in our room." Captain Mortimer reached the bottom of the stairs and walked over to where she stood immobilized by Gerald Dawson.

Dawson sneered.

"Didn't take you long to find another man to warm your bed, did it?"

Jenny remained frozen, utterly paralyzed. She didn't even struggle to get away from Dawson's grasp. She was mortified. What would Captain Mortimer think of her now? She could tell nothing from his expression. He smiled in a friendly manner to Dawson and held out her hairbrush to her. When she took it, he held his hand out to Dawson.

"Captain Mortimer," he said, introducing himself.

"Gerald Dawson." Dawson shook Mortimer's hand without relinquishing his hold on Jenny's arm. "I'm Miss Carlisle's betrothed."

Jenny flinched and looked away.

"Nice to meet you," Mortimer said, still the picture of civility and politesse.

"I'm sure it is." Dawson emitted a snide laugh. "Hope you enjoyed her last night, but she's mine and I'll be taking her with me now." He pulled Jenny toward the door. "Get in the curricle," he ordered.

Jenny resisted. Finally, the fear changed from paralysis to action. She pulled her arm, trying to get free of Dawson's grasp. His grip became tighter and he pulled with more force.

The hairbrush in her hand was heavy, with a solid, silver back. She lifted it to bash against Dawson's imprisoning hand, but before she had the chance, Captain Mortimer's cane lashed down on Dawson's arm. He cried out in pain and released his grasp. Suddenly free, Jenny stumbled backward. Captain Mortimer inserted himself between her and Dawson.

"I believe, sir, that the lady is not willing to leave with you. I suggest you get in your curricle yourself and return home."

"You have no right," Dawson stammered. "We are betrothed. We were to speak our vows yesterday morning before all of London. She belongs to me."

Calmly, Captain Mortimer turned to Jenny. "Do you wish to leave with this man?"

Jenny shook her head no.

"Is there a problem, Captain?" Nelson said from the open doorway.

"Nelson, please escort Mr. Dawson here to his curricle and see that he goes on his way."

Grabbing Dawson by the arm, Nelson effortlessly

dragged him out of the inn. Dawson must have said something Nelson took exception to because he punched Dawson in the belly, causing him to double over. Without waiting for Dawson to recover, Nelson hoisted him into the seat of the waiting curricle. As the horses pranced, Nelson pulled Dawson down by his collar so he could speak to him face to face.

When Nelson released him, Dawson picked up the reins, gave one last look at the inn doorway as though he could see her where she stood inside, then slapped the backs of the horses and the curricle set off.

Jenny let out the breath she'd been holding. She turned to say her thanks to Captain Mortimer, but the sound of wheels on cobbles brought her attention back to the inn yard. The coach followed Dawson's curricle out of the yard and headed speedily down the road toward Bath.

"The coach!" she cried. "I've missed the coach!"

It broke her. Jenny put her hands over her face and let out a sob. She had no money. She had no way to get to her Aunt Julia in Bath. Gerald Dawson would come back for her as soon as he saw that Captain Mortimer had gone on his way. She had no hope of escape. He would cart her back to London and force her to marry him even though he knew how much she loathed him.

A strong arm came around her and gently stroked her back. She leaned into Captain Mortimer's shoulder and took the comfort he offered.

"I can't imagine what you must think of me," she whispered into his coat. He put his hand under her chin and lifted her face to look at him.

"I think you are a very brave girl."

She gave him a watery smile. "I'm hardly feeling very brave right now."

Gently, he wiped a tear from her cheek with his

thumb. "Sometimes it takes the greatest courage to know when to retreat. I think you were wise in choosing not to marry that man."

Relief flooded through her. Finally, someone saw her side. Someone who didn't judge and condemn her. Of course, he didn't know everything. He would probably treat her with the same disdain that her father did, the same cold disgust if he knew her own foolishness had brought her here.

It seemed impossible to her now that she hadn't seen Dawson's cruelty the first time she met him. Captain Mortimer had not been deluded by him at all, he'd seen Dawson's true character immediately. But she, foolish girl, had actually liked Gerald Dawson and enjoyed his company. She deserved her fate if for no other reason than her own dimwittedness.

"Nelson and I shall take you up to Bath with us," Mortimer said. "It is only a short detour from Fairleigh."

"Captain," she started to object, then thought better of it. If she misjudged Captain Mortimer in the same way she'd misjudged Gerald Dawson, then so be it. She had only two choices. Wait here for Dawson to come back for her or take her chances with the captain and his batman and hope for the best. Hope that they were truly the gentlemen they appeared to be. "Thank you." She accepted his offer graciously.

∞∞∞∞

Nelson chose to ride on the high seat of the carriage with the driver, leaving the interior of the closed carriage for Mortimer and Jenny to share. Jenny sat stiffly on the seat, staring fixedly out the window. She was trying to make herself as small as possible, much as she'd done last night in the taproom. If she could become invisible, he was sure she would do it.

Mortimer's leg pained him. Every bump in the road shot agony up his thigh. It hadn't hurt this much when the damned lead ball had shot into him.

He kept his flask handy and sipped brandy constantly, but it wasn't easing the pain. Perhaps because every time he lifted the flask to his lips, Jenny flinched.

She was petrified. Waiting, he supposed, for him to accost her or make demands of her. He was in too much discomfort to try to reassure her, so they rode in silence through the morning.

At midday they stopped at a post house to take luncheon. Nelson helped Jenny down. To Mortimer's embarrassment, Nelson assisted him in disembarking as well, lifting him out of the carriage as if he were a child. Mortimer wobbled a bit, finally feeling the effects of the brandy. Opting to remain outdoors to enjoy the warm July day while Nelson and Jenny went inside to procure their meal, he unsteadily made his way to a bench handily placed under a shade tree.

Mortimer rubbed his thigh where the lead ball remained lodged. It seemed wrong to have this remnant of his violent past here in the peaceful English countryside. Here in this garden, it felt as if war didn't exist, as though battles had never been fought, as if men weren't dying still. He breathed in the fragrance of flowers, listened to the hum of bees, savored the sweet warmth of the sun and felt out of place.

He hadn't known peace in ten years. He didn't know what to do with it.

He had his eyes closed when he heard someone approach. The sound had his hand tightening its grip on the handle of his cane until he remembered no enemy surrounded him. He opened his eyes and watched Jenny carry a cloth-covered basket and water pitcher over to where he sat.

"I've brought your lunch for you." She set the basket down on the bench next to him then sat on the other side of it. "Mr. Nelson is having an ale inside and gossiping with some of the local men."

Mortimer knew Nelson had purposely sent her on this errand to keep her out of the taproom. It was no place for a lady.

She was a lady, Mortimer had no doubt about that. He didn't know much about Miss Carlisle, but everything about her bespoke quality and gentility. How she had become associated with a man the likes of Dawson he couldn't fathom, but at least she had sense enough to run far and fast before becoming leg shackled to the oaf.

She handed him some bread and cheese and he took it gratefully. She poured him a cup of water from the pitcher. He drank thirstily and she refilled it.

She wasn't eating.

"Did you eat inside?" he asked, though he knew she hadn't.

"Yes," she said. But she wasn't a very good liar. No better than at breakfast when she'd told him she didn't know where she'd be staying in Bath. She had lied then and she lied now. He broke off a chunk of bread and gave it to her. "Eat."

"I'm fine, really. Still full from that wonderful breakfast you served me."

"Is it pride or stubbornness?" he asked bluntly.

Jenny smiled. "Stubbornness, most definitely." She took the bread and helped herself to a piece of cheese from the basket.

"Your leg is bothering you." She said it as a statement.

"My leg is always bothering me."

"How long ago were you wounded?"

It wasn't his favorite topic, but at least it had her

talking. "Four months. I spent several weeks in field hospitals while they decided whether I would live or die. The physicians contemplated cutting off my leg, but the location of the wound made that untenable. They were unable to remove the ball, so I expect I will have to learn to live with the discomfort. It took awhile for me to gain enough strength to make the journey home."

He tried to make light of it, but her expression told him she knew it had been an ordeal.

"I've read accounts of soldiers dying from infection and disease, so I know how remarkable it is that you survived at all. I am very grateful that you did and that you are returning home at this time. It was my good fortune for us to meet."

"Miss Carlisle, I don't mean to pry and you don't have to tell me anything if you don't want to, but how did you come to be a runaway bride?"

Jenny turned away from him and looked at the sky, the trees, the flowers in the garden that fronted the posting house. Anywhere but at him. He didn't think she would tell him, or perhaps she was trying to decide what she could tell him. He wasn't prepared for the truth, but he wasn't surprised by it.

"Mr. Dawson was one of my suitors. I am in my first Season, and while I am not a diamond of the first water, I had my share of admirers. Mr. Dawson was charming and amiable. He called on me on several occasions. We never spent any time alone together, he was just one of several young men to show an interest in me.

"A gentleman named Conrad Nash won my preference. Hating to disappoint any of my other suitors, and not wanting them to feel snubbed, I felt honor bound to inform each young man that I no longer desired his courtship.

"All of them were perfectly amenable when I pulled

them aside for a quiet word, wishing me happy and thanking me for telling them personally.

"All except Mr. Dawson.

"When I stepped outside on the terrace with him at the Attleborough's ball and told him I had found the man I hoped to marry and that I could no longer entertain his suit, he changed from an agreeable young man to a monster in the blink of an eye."

She hesitated and Mortimer wanted to tell her to stop. She didn't have to say anymore, he could speculate on the rest. She continued before he opened his mouth.

"He dragged me down the terrace steps to the bushes. He pushed me to the ground and he. . .he. . ."

Mortimer reached out and took her hand in his.

"You needn't say more. What he did was despicable. Why did your father not call him out?"

Tears streamed down her cheeks.

"I was so ashamed, so embarrassed, I didn't tell anyone what happened. When he was finished, Gerald, Mr. Dawson, dragged me to our carriage and sent me home. I learned afterward that he returned to the ball and told everyone that I'd taken ill and left early.

"I was so relieved to escape him, I went home willingly. I crawled into bed, shocked by what had happened and hoping, I suppose, that when I awoke I would discover it had all been a bad dream. My mother poked her head in to check on me when she came home from the ball, but I feigned sleep. I didn't want to talk to anyone, could not tell anyone. I didn't want to believe it had happened.

"The next morning, my father called me down to his study. Gerald stood by the windows smiling smugly. Father said he'd accepted Gerald's offer to marry me. I tried to argue, but Father would have none of it."

She squeezed his hand so tightly he'd lost feeling in it,

but he let her hold on. He wanted to put his hand over her mouth, to keep her from having to relive the awful pain.

"I told Father that he'd forced himself on me and Father said 'I know. It's your own fault, now you have to live with the consequences.' I didn't know what to do. The banns were posted and the wedding day set. I went through it all like a sleepwalker living in a nightmare. Then yesterday morning, I couldn't go through with it. I ran."

"Bravo, Jenny. Bravo."

Jenny looked up at him. He smiled at her, like he was proud of her. His blue eyes shone with tears of his own.

"You don't think I'm despicable?"

"I think you are very brave."

Nelson and the carriage driver came out then, and they soon were on their way. The atmosphere inside the carriage eased during the afternoon's journey.

For the first time since that awful night, Jenny felt she wasn't alone.

They arrived in Bath just before it became full dark. Jenny had the horrifying thought that Aunt Julia might not be at home, but as soon as Nelson banged the knocker, Julia burst out the front door to greet her.

"Jenny child, what a delight to see you," Julia cried. "I didn't expect you to come to Bath on your wedding trip. This must be your new husband."

Julia hugged her then turned to bestow a hug on Mortimer who stood protectively at her side.

"This is Captain Mortimer," Jenny tried to explain to her enthusiastic aunt. "He's not my husband. I didn't get married. Aunt Julia, I need a place to stay until I can sort things out."

"Didn't get married, whyever not?"

"Perhaps you had best go inside and talk," Mortimer

suggested. "Miss Carlisle, I leave you in your aunt's good hands." He took Jenny's hands in his and brushed a soft kiss on them. "You have my direction. Feel free to call on me if you ever need anything. Anything. Ever."

Jenny felt the warmth of his affection and it gave her courage.

"Thank you, Captain. I'll be fine." She smiled at him.

Mortimer stood beside the carriage until Jenny and her aunt were safely enclosed inside the house.

"Let's go home, Nelson." Mortimer and his batman climbed into the carriage. They had another two hours to go before reaching Fairleigh.

"Will she be all right do you think?" Nelson asked when they were underway.

"I hope so," Mortimer replied. "I hated leaving her without some assurance of her fate. I believe I shall be returning to Bath in a few days, Nelson. Just to make sure she is safe. What did that fool Dawson say to you when you escorted him to his curricle?"

"The bastard made an unseemly remark about you and Miss Carlisle. I would have taken offense even if I hadn't known it to be completely untrue, knowing as I did where you slept last night. Miss Carlisle is a lady, anyone can see that."

"That she is, Nelson. That she is."

∞∞∞∞

Julia called for a bath, and while Jenny soaked, interrogated her.

"I only received the letter from your mother the other day telling me you were to be married yesterday. What are you doing here? Who brought you if not your husband? What have you done Jenny?"

"I decided Mr. Dawson and I would not suit. No one

would listen to me. Mother and Father were insistent that I go through with the marriage. I saw no other recourse but to get away. Please, Aunt Julia, will you help me convince them that marrying Mr. Dawson would be the worst possible fate for me?"

"I don't know Mr. Dawson at all, or anything about his people, but surely your father would not have approved the match if he didn't think it the best thing for you. I know it's your first Season, Jenny, but you aren't a child any longer. You're nearly twenty. It would be best for you to be settled." Julia reached for a towel and helped Jenny out of the bathtub. "Now, does your decision not to marry Mr. Dawson have anything to do with Captain Mortimer?"

"Not at all. I only met Captain Mortimer last night. He came to my rescue when the coach had to stop unexpectedly at an inn. My reason for not marrying Mr. Dawson is personal." Wrapped in a warm robe, Jenny let down her hair. Julia picked up a brush and brushed it with soft, soothing strokes. Jenny felt safe and warm. And hopeful. The nightmare of the past weeks seemed like pure imagination. As if it had never happened.

"What personal reason?" Julia wasn't satisfied with her explanation, but Jenny didn't want to tell her the entire story. Too many people knew of her indiscretion already. Jenny didn't want to risk Julia turning her back on her as her parents had done.

"I fear that Mr. Dawson is a violent man," Jenny said. "I think he would be a cruel husband."

Julia's hand stilled. "Your father would not wed you to a violent man. He loves you too much."

Jenny had always believed that, but now she knew the truth. Her father loved his position in Society and his reputation far more than he loved her. He had willingly sold her to a vicious fortune hunter rather than face

Society's censure.

Jenny turned to face Julia. "Father will likely be very angry with me. Will you stand by me?"

Julia gave her a reassuring smile. "Of course, dear." She said it with less confidence than Jenny would have liked, but at least she had one ally.

No, she had two. Captain Mortimer was her ally as well, though she would likely never see him again. Knowing that he had not repudiated her gave her strength.

A strength she would need in the days ahead..

THREE

Fairleigh slept when they arrived. Mortimer directed the driver to the stables and he and Nelson assisted the man in grooming the horses and getting them settled. The driver would be making the return trip to London in the morning with the hired carriage. Mortimer commended the man on his handling of the team and showed him where to sleep.

The house was locked up tight for the night. Rather than waking the staff with his unexpected arrival, Mortimer and Nelson bedded down in the groom's quarters as well. One more night without that soft feather bed he'd been dreaming about since he'd been wounded. One more night a soldier. Tomorrow, he would become a gentleman.

Mortimer fell asleep thinking about Jenny Carlisle, wondering how she fared. He would check on her as soon as he settled things here.

∞∞∞∞

The next morning, Aunt Julia took Jenny shopping. "I

can't believe this is all you brought with you!" she'd exclaimed when she unpacked Jenny's single bag.

"I packed a bit hurriedly," Jenny demurred.

They visited the best shops in Bath. Jenny tried to restrain Julia for she didn't know how she would pay for any purchases.

"We'll have them send the bills to your father," Julia decreed.

"No, Aunt Julia, absolutely not. I am not in Father's good graces right now, I won't give him more reason to be angry with me."

In the end, they had the bills sent to Julia. Since, as Julia pointed out, Mr. Carlisle paid her a quarterly allowance, it amounted to the same thing.

Bath bustled during the summer with many more people than Jenny had expected. She had thought all of Society still in London, but much of it had already removed itself to Bath. And with that removal came all the gossip from Town.

Jenny's aborted wedding became a prime topic of conversation. Adding to her misery, Dawson had started vile rumors about her and Captain Mortimer. Everywhere she went, stares and whispers accosted her. She couldn't believe how quickly word had spread, and to her distress, she found herself a pariah in Bath Society.

The following afternoon, when she and Julia stopped in Granby's for an ice, they were given the cut direct. Even Julia's friends treated her frostily.

Julia lacked her usual ebullience when they returned home. She suggested that Jenny go upstairs and rest, but Jenny insisted they talk.

"I think I should leave," Jenny said. "I'm making life difficult for you."

"Nonsense, nonsense, my dear," Julia said without much conviction. "I must ask you to tell me, is there any credence to these rumors about you and Captain Mortimer?"

Jenny wanted to scream in frustration. She'd made one mistake that evening in London, and now her entire world had fallen in around her. Not only had she ruined her own life, but the lives of so many others. Captain Mortimer's reputation was being tainted by his association with her when he'd only sought to offer her kindness. Aunt Julia, too, was suffering for her mistake.

The only person not harmed was the person responsible for all of it, Gerald Dawson. Society painted him with sympathetic strokes, poor man left standing at the altar, jilted by a hussy who couldn't wait to run off with another man.

"Captain Mortimer showed me kindness, nothing more," Jenny explained for what seemed like the hundredth time as she realized it didn't matter what she said or how often she denied it.

She was ruined. And her ruin infected all those around her.

"I'll write to my friend Caroline," Jenny offered. "Perhaps she will invite me for a visit."

Caroline had married a country squire and lived quietly in a remote corner of Cornwall. Farther from the wagging tongues of Society's matrons Jenny couldn't imagine being.

"I'll go up to my room now and compose my letter."

∞∞∞∞

Mortimer had intended to return to Bath as soon as he had himself settled at Fairleigh, but his first morning home found him sick with fever. His wound, infected again, turned an angry red and drained pus. It never completely healed because of the lead ball still lodged at the very top of his thigh. It had nearly castrated him—had for all intents and purposes.

That was the least of his worries, however, as he took to his bed and sweated out the fever. His illness had one saving grace—it delayed his first interview with his mother for several days. She assiduously avoided his sick room and sent all communications through Nelson, who tended him as nursemaid.

His third morning home, he managed to make it down to breakfast though he was still pale and kitten weak. He knew the girl seated at the table must be his sister Abigail because she had the Mortimer eyes and chestnut hair, but he didn't know her, hadn't seen her since she was a child. She was a young woman now, dressed modestly in a pale green day dress. She watched him warily as he entered, walking awkwardly and heavily leaning on his cane.

"Good morning, Abigail," he greeted her. He took the seat at the head of the table and waited for a servant to bring him a plate from the sideboard. Normally, he would have served himself, but he could not stand for long and would be returning to his room as soon as he completed his morning obligations.

"It's good to have you home, brother," she said formally. She looked down at her plate then and whispered, "We've missed you."

He wanted to say he'd missed her, too, but in truth he'd barely given her a thought in all the years he'd been gone. He had neglected her and his responsibilities to her in the years since Elliot died. He should have taken an interest in her education and her future.

He had left it all to their mother, just as he'd left her the responsibility of running Fairleigh. Would his mother resent him coming home now to take over from her, or would she see it as relief? He had yet to speak with her.

Mortimer's relationship with his mother had never

been good. She'd doted on Elliot and had ignored him. She always took his father's side whenever the old tyrant disciplined him—usually with a riding crop, but sometimes with his bare fists. To Mortimer's knowledge, his father had never raised a hand to anyone but him. He never knew why he caused such violence in the man, but for as long as he could remember, he had evoked it.

He had never intentionally tried to misbehave, but nothing he ever did was good enough. He wasn't as smart as Elliot, so he got beaten. He wasn't as good a rider as Elliot, so he received a slap across his cheek. He tried to avoid his father by spending his days out of doors but was punished for not being at home.

Going to school saved him. Unlike most of the boys, he didn't long for home. The discipline that the headmasters doled out, which most of the young men found harsh, was feather light compared to what Mortimer had endured at home.

Looking at Abigail now, he wondered if he'd done her a disservice by leaving her at the hands of their parents. She seemed not to have suffered. She looked healthy and self-assured.

"Will you be staying at home?" Abigail asked timidly.

"Yes." He hadn't realized until that moment it was true. He was a man now, not a frightened boy. His father was dead and buried, may he reside in Hell. Mortimer had no reason to run any longer.

He looked around the dining room, trying to comprehend that it belonged to him now. The rich woodwork, the paintings that decorated the walls, the chandelier that hung over the solid mahogany table. It all belonged to him.

His entire life he had felt like a stranger in this house, like a changeling who didn't really belong. Now he was master of it all.

His mother joined them then, and Mortimer saw her as he had never seen her before—as a small, bird-like woman who had grown old in the years he'd been gone. She gave him a pointed look when he remained sitting.

"Forgive me, madam, but I am unable to stand very easily." He felt embarrassed at having to explain himself. Once again, he felt like the small boy who could never do anything right.

"Of course, your leg wound." She said it as if it were of no consequence. "If you had returned home when Elliot died, you would not have suffered it." There. Welcome home.

Letitia Mortimer may have been small in stature, but she held herself ramrod straight so she appeared taller. She was exact in everything she did, always requiring things to be just so. She knew the correct way to behave in every situation and never shied from telling others how to act.

"Sit up straight, Abigail," she instructed. Abigail threw Mortimer an embarrassed glance. He winked at her and she smiled. Perhaps he had an ally after all.

"I shall ask Mr. Godfrey, the steward, to join us in the study so we may go over the accounts. I assume you will be taking over management of the estate?"

He couldn't tell if she was sorry to be giving up control or reprimanding him for shirking his duties for so long.

"I will manage things from now on," he told her.

As an officer in the military, he had commanded troops in battle. He had never felt as intimidated on the field as he felt in the presence of this small woman, his mother. He had always wanted her respect and approval but had done nothing but win her disappointment.

As a military man, he knew that some battles could not be won. For the first time in his life, he realized that this was one of them. He, however, was no longer the conquered, but the conquering army. And his mother knew it. She could try her best to undermine him, to make him feel inadequate, but they both knew the balance of power had shifted. He was in control now. She had no power over him any longer.

Mortimer smiled at his mother. "Do have some breakfast, Mother. Then, before we meet with Mr. Godfrey, I would like it if you and I could have a talk."

The time had come to forge a new relationship with this woman.

∞∞∞∞

Society loved a scandal and, once Jenny stopped accompanying her, Julia reaped the benefits of Jenny's scandalous behavior by receiving more invitations than ever before. Jenny, however, was persona non grata. Thus, on her fourth morning in Bath, she had gone out early to the lending library to procure more novels to read in the evening when Julia was out.

Jenny had settled into a routine that suited her. She had always enjoyed the quieter pastimes of the country even though she had been enjoying the routs and balls of a London Season. It was no hardship for her to live a quiet life away from the social events that most young women her age found so essential.

At least, that's what she told herself. If she were completely honest, she'd have to admit that inside she seethed with resentment. She had done nothing to warrant the harsh treatment she was receiving.

Captain Mortimer had been proud of her for refusing to marry Mr. Dawson. He had seen immediately what kind of man he was. Yet, Mr. Dawson remained in Society's good graces while she was ostracized.

She had made a mistake in going out alone on the terrace with Mr. Dawson, that she knew, but it was a mistake borne of kindness. She hadn't wanted to hurt his feelings. What a fool she'd been. He had no feelings other than selfishness and greed. Had he been a gentleman, being alone with him for a few moments would not have even been noted.

But Dawson was no gentleman. He had wanted something and he'd taken it. He'd used whatever means at his disposal to get her to marry him because, as she learned too late, he needed her money. Mr. Dawson was penniless. The income he was reputed to have had been recklessly spent. He was deeply in debt. He had courted her only because her father was wealthy, and she would bring a good dowry. When she'd rejected him, he took her by force.

But no one censured Mr. Dawson. He could continue being accepted into the best drawing rooms, could continue courting other innocent, vulnerable young women. While she received the cut direct.

All her life, Jenny had strived to do the right thing. She was never daring, never demanding. She hadn't even minded waiting to have her first season with her younger sister Delia. Their parents did not embrace Town life as a rule and only wanted to go to the trouble and expense of one Season. They had hoped to marry off both girls the same year and be done with it.

Her father had purchased a lovely Town house in Mayfair. With her mother and sister Delia, she had visited modistes and milliners on Bond Street. Jenny had been having a marvelous time.

Dutifully, she did her best to find suitable young men to attend her. She was not a great beauty, she knew, and had a shy, quiet personality. Her sister was more lively and attracted far more attention. Still, Jenny had been courted by four suitors and she had especially liked Conrad Nash.

Jenny shifted the three books she'd checked out under her arm as she crossed Broad Street heading toward Julia's house. The maid Julia had sent along to accompany her hurried to catch up. But the more Jenny thought about that awful day, the faster she walked. The awful day when, after her engagement to Mr. Dawson had been announced, she'd seen Conrad Nash at the theater. He'd looked at her with such longing and such loathing.

She wondered if she should have told him the truth. Would he have defended her honor? Her father hadn't. Her father had made her feel that she had acted so dishonorably she was beyond defense.

Captain Mortimer would have defended her. He would not allow any daughter of his to suffer such humiliation and disgrace.

She rounded the corner to Julia's street and saw a carriage parked in front of the house. For a moment, her heart surged as she thought it might be Captain Mortimer coming to pay a call. But then she saw the design on the carriage doors and knew to whom it belonged.

She was surprised it had taken him four days to come after her. The confrontation was unavoidable, she knew, but she wished she could keep walking. A fleeting hope kept pace with her as she climbed the front steps. Maybe this time he would see her side.

From the entry hall, Jenny watched her father pace before the cold fireplace.

Douglas Carlisle was a dour man. A man of business. Many in Society looked down their noses at him, especially those who were indebted to him. He'd built a sizeable fortune from coal mines and factories.

Though not nobility, his family tree held a few noble branches and his lineage was impeccable, as he was always quick to point out. He'd clawed his way up from middle class to gentry and by God he'd let nothing steal it from him.

Especially not a recalcitrant daughter.

Poor Father, his one failing in life was not producing a son to pass his inheritance on to. He'd been cursed with daughters.

She knew he expected her sister Delia to cause him problems, not her. Delia was the stubborn, headstrong one, not Jenny. Jenny had always been his delight—meek and biddable, kind to a fault, always bringing home strays—animals and people. Jenny had been his favorite.

Which was why their estrangement hurt so much. She'd seen his anger directed at others, but never at her.

In his eyes she'd betrayed him with a man he did not find worthy to call son. She'd put him in the position of having to appease a scoundrel in order to protect his reputation. A businessman was nothing without his reputation—a precept he'd drummed into her all her life.

His biddable daughter had become a harlot and a rebel. She'd brought him disappointment and shame.

As she watched, he rubbed his hand across his brow. Jenny saw the anguish in his face and wanted to comfort him. She had never meant to cause him pain. She loved her father and had always tried to please him.

She took a step forward, wanting to run to him, put her arms around him, tell him it would be all right. They'd get through this crisis together.

Her movement drew his attention.

When he saw her, anguish turned to disgust. Not here to forgive her, then. Rather, here to control her as he always had.

"Pack your things, Jenny, we are returning to London."

"Good day to you, too, Father." Jenny entered the

room. "Surely you want to rest at least a day before making the journey home."

"I arrived yesterday and stayed with a friend of mine on High Street. He reluctantly shared with me the latest rumors about you. What are you doing, girl? Why are you behaving this way?"

"I'm not behaving in any way."

"I don't even know if Dawson will still have you, but if you come back and go through with the marriage, people will forget the scandal and accept you again."

"I won't marry Gerald Dawson."

"You have to," her father shouted, turning red in the face. "I agreed to it, we have a contract. If you don't marry him, he can take me to court for breach of contract. Do you want to see that happen? Think about your mother and sister. Have you no care for anyone but yourself? I never knew you to be a selfish girl, Jenny."

Jenny wearily put her books on the table in Julia's drawing room. She removed her hat and set it beside the books. This interview would be no different from all the others. How many times had she tried to convince her father during the weeks leading up to the wedding that marrying Gerald Dawson was a mistake?

"You agreed to it, Father, I never did."

"You put yourself in the position that caused this scandal. You admitted going out on the terrace alone with the man when you knew very well you should have been chaperoned. I don't condone what Dawson did, but at least he's willing to make it right. He's made an honest offer of marriage. You're ruined for anyone else, you know that. It's your only option."

"No." Jenny stiffened her spine, standing as tall as she could, and faced her father's anger. "I will not marry Gerald Dawson."

"Then you are no longer my daughter." The

pronouncement rang in the room. He may not have intended to say it, but now that he had, she knew he would not take it back. "You either come with me now or I am through with you."

"Do what you must, Father." Jenny's stomach dropped as she realized the enormity of what she was doing. She would never be able to go back home, never see her sister or mother again. Was it worth it? Should she just accept the fate that had been dealt her and marry the odious man?

No. She could not. She would die if she had to spend one night with him.

They stood staring at each other, neither knowing what to say.

"Very well, then." Father finally broke the impasse. "But don't think you can stay here with Julia. If she keeps you, I will cut off her allowance. She's dependent on me as well, you know."

Jenny hadn't known, or she hadn't given it much thought. She'd always assumed Julia had been left a small income by her late husband that her father's allowance merely supplemented. Jenny looked at Julia who had been sitting quietly throughout the entire exchange.

"Aunt Julia?" Jenny could see the answer in the older woman's eyes.

Jenny turned and left the room. She had to act immediately or she would lose her resolve. She went to the room Julia had given her and packed her meager belongings. She took the two dresses Julia had bought for her, surely her father would not begrudge her them. Carrying her bag, Jenny walked out the front door. She had no idea where to go.

She checked her pockets and her purse. She had not a farthing to her name. She was homeless. Destitute.

She started walking.

How many days, she wondered, would it take her to walk from Bath to Cornwall to visit Caroline? Caroline was the only person in the whole of England she could think of who would welcome her.

Jenny felt utterly alone. She wanted to cry, but she was too stunned to do so.

Hope still dwelled in her. She listened for her father's carriage. Perhaps when he realized the lengths to which she would go he would renege and come after her. She reached the corner and turned left on Broad Street, retracing her steps to the lending library. She could at least sit there for the day and read. They closed at three o'clock though, and she didn't know what she would do then.

She had almost reached the library steps when she felt the slip of paper in her pocket. Captain Mortimer's direction. He'd said Fairleigh was twenty miles north of Bath. She could walk twenty miles in a day, couldn't she?

She could try.

She stopped and asked a street vendor for the best way to go. Armed with his directions, Jenny set off. Completely on her own.

FOUR

Mortimer lit the desk lamp and stretched before resuming his seat. Even though he'd slept most of the afternoon, fatigue clawed at him. He still felt poorly, but refused to give in to it. He had too much to do.

He'd apologized to his mother that morning for leaving her the task of running Fairleigh for so long but assured her she was relieved of those duties. She had not been pleased. He'd met for two hours with Mr. Godfrey, the steward, who had seemed competent and honest. Then he'd crawled to his bed, unable to keep his eyes open any longer.

Dinner had been formal and uncomfortable. His mother barely spoke to him. Abigail attempted lighthearted conversation, but she received no cooperation from her dinner companions and finally lapsed into silence herself. Mortimer had retreated to the library immediately after the meal to begin reviewing the estate accounts.

Overall, the property was prosperous and running efficiently. Tomorrow he would take the family carriage out and inspect what he could. How he longed to be able to ride horseback across the fields so he could really assess the situation.

He reviewed again the notes he'd taken during his interview with Mr. Godfrey. They had some fields in wheat and some in barley. They had milk cows and cattle for beef. They had sheep, some for wool, others for slaughter. They'd had a good harvest the previous year and expected a similarly good harvest this fall.

Mortimer rubbed his tired eyes and tried again to focus on the accounts. They made him want to sleep. Perhaps he had dismissed his mother too soon. He had no liking for this work. He would rather be out in the fields helping the tenants with the planting than sitting at his desk adding numbers.

He was a soldier, not a gentleman farmer.

As if to taunt him, a shot of pain coursed through his thigh. No, he was no longer a soldier. So he had better adapt and learn how to be a gentleman farmer. He turned his attention again to the miserable accounts that made his eyes bleary.

After another hour, he caught himself nodding in his chair. It was no use. It was time to seek his bed.

He had reached the foot of the stairs when the door knocker sounded. Visitors were uncommon at Fairleigh, especially at this time of night, so they kept no porter. The butler had already retired, Mortimer assumed, so he went to answer the door himself. Probably not proper for a country gentleman to do, he thought, but he was too accustomed to the expediency of the battlefield where etiquette often took second place to necessity.

Mortimer opened the door and Jenny Carlisle launched herself into his arms.

"Oh, Captain Mortimer, I am so relieved to find you at home." She cried great gasping sobs.

"Whatever has happened?" He led her back to the

library and relit the lamp he had so recently put out. Settling her in a chair, he went to the brandy cart and poured her a goblet. "Drink this," he said, handing her the glass. She gulped it down then coughed as it burned its way down her throat. But at least she stopped crying.

"I am so sorry to turn up on your doorstep this way, but I had no place else to go." Mortimer refilled her brandy glass and poured one for himself as she told him about the altercation with her father. "I never believed that he would not come after me. I kept looking behind me hoping to find him there. But he never came."

Mortimer smiled even though the situation was certainly severe.

"Perhaps it is from your father that you inherited your stubbornness," he said.

"You think I'm wrong?" She looked devastated at the thought.

"No." Mortimer went to the bell pull and rang for a servant. "Let's get you settled for the night, and we'll sort things out in the morning." He would write to her father and let him know she was safe. Beyond that, he had no idea what to do with her.

One thing was sure. He would not allow her to marry Gerald Dawson. The man was a brute and a conniver who would crush her.

∞∞∞∞

Jenny sank gratefully into bed. Her feet throbbed and every muscle in her body ached. Captain Mortimer's twenty miles had seemed more like fifty. She thought her journey would never end.

Doubts had assailed her every step of the way. If Captain Mortimer thought she should return home and marry Mr. Dawson, she decided she would do it. She hadn't realized how disappointed she would feel if he hadn't taken her side.

But he had taken her side and with such confidence that she knew immediate relief.

Jenny rolled onto her side, trying to find a more comfortable position. It seemed like she ached over every inch of her body. Her journey had been an ordeal, both physically and mentally. She realized once again how vulnerable unprotected women were out in the world. Men had offered to take her up in their wagons and carriages in exchange for favors she refused to give. She'd been leered at and shouted at and nearly run off the road on several occasions.

She had begged for water and a crust of bread. She realized how easy it would be to fall prey to unscrupulous scoundrels. She had never felt so relieved in her life as she had when she finally came upon the gate to Fairleigh. When Captain Mortimer opened the door to her, she'd nearly fainted with relief.

Jenny's eyes drifted closed as she relaxed into the comfortable bed. She was safe now. Captain Mortimer would keep her safe.

∞∞∞∞∞

"I have hired Miss Carlisle to be Abigail's companion," Mortimer announced at breakfast the next morning. "That is, if you accept the post, Miss Carlisle."

Jenny had been awakened by a servant and invited to join the family for breakfast. She'd hastily made her toilette and donned the least wrinkled of the three dresses she had with her.

The servant led her to a formal dining room where Captain Mortimer introduced her to Mrs. Mortimer, his mother, and his sister, Abigail.

Jenny looked at Abigail, a girl of about seventeen, very close to her own sister Delia's age. Like Delia, Abigail had the fresh-faced look of innocence. Had she herself ever been that young?

Jenny looked at Captain Mortimer. Did he realize what he was doing? Hiring her to be companion to Abigail was like hiring a member of the demimonde to act as duenna. A companion was charged with safeguarding the morals of her charge. Who but Captain Mortimer would think her capable of such a task?

Certainly not the girl's mother, if Jenny read her expression correctly. Mrs. Mortimer did not appear at all pleased with the captain's pronouncement.

Jenny could certainly understand the woman's reluctance to accept a complete stranger into her household. While Jenny sympathized with Mrs. Mortimer's concerns, she was not about to turn the position down.

This morning, Jenny was willing to accept any offer Captain Mortimer made. She did not want to find herself on the road again, penniless and alone, with no destination in mind.

"I would be happy to accept," Jenny said. Mrs. Mortimer drew in a sharp breath and Jenny faltered. "If it is acceptable to Abigail and Mrs. Mortimer," she added.

"Do you have references?" Mrs. Mortimer took the opening Jenny had given her.

"I am her reference," Mortimer stated. "I know Miss Carlisle to be of good family and high moral character."

Jenny wanted to argue at his assertion, knowing full well how flawed her moral character really was.

"She's too young," Mrs. Mortimer declared.

"She is not much older than Abigail, that's true," Mortimer countered. "Which is all the more reason why I chose her. Abigail needs a companion who can also act as her friend."

Mrs. Mortimer was warming up to present another argument when Mortimer superseded her.

"What do you say, Abigail? Would you like Miss Carlisle to be your companion?"

Abigail smiled warmly at her brother then turned the smile on Jenny.

"Oh, yes, Richard. Thank you."

"It's settled then. Miss Carlisle, please join me in the library after breakfast so we can go over the details of your position."

∞∞∞∞

"I'm sorry, I didn't mean to ambush you like that, but it seemed like the perfect solution to your problem and a boon to Abigail as well. My mother, as you saw, can be difficult. Abigail has led a rather isolated existence here at Fairleigh, I'm afraid. I would like to change that."

"Captain Mortimer, you must not be ignorant of what you are doing. By hiring me as companion to Abigail, you may be tainting her with my scandal. Fairleigh is not very far from Bath, and believe me, all Bath is aware of my scandalous behavior."

"All you have done is refuse to marry a man you have decided will not suit. Your behavior may be considered impetuous, but certainly not scandalous. I doubt even Dawson would put it about that you and he had acted in any way improperly."

"He has put it out that you and I have acted improperly." Jenny hated to have to tell him, but he deserved to know the truth. Rumors abounded in Bath about her and Captain Mortimer sharing a room at the inn.

"Ah, but I have witnesses who can dispel any rumors

he has started. Nelson, the hostlers, and grooms all know that I slept in the stable that night and you were alone in that room. I'll send Nelson to Bath today to set the story aright. I will also have him deliver a letter to your father letting him know where you are and that you are safe. And that you are properly employed and no longer his responsibility. He can tell Dawson to go to Hell." Mortimer apologized for cursing.

At that moment, Jenny fell in love. Captain Mortimer was her hero. She could understand how men eagerly followed him into battle. She would be willing to lay down her life for him. He made her feel safe and strong and powerful.

Experience had taught her that she was none of those things. While she admired Captain Mortimer's confidence, she knew how difficult it would be to repair her damaged reputation. And she knew how easily her blackened reputation could stain Abigail's.

"I will stay only as long as it does no harm to anyone else, especially you or Abigail."

Mortimer agreed only to appease her conscience. If only she knew how little he cared what Society said. Scandals meant little after the horrors of war. He judged men, and women, by their characters, not their reputation. He had taken the measure of Jenny's character that night at the inn when, frightened and alone, she had looked him squarely in the eye and told him, ever so politely of course, what he could do with his room.

Society matrons could wag their tongues about her all they wanted, but he knew Jenny Carlisle to be of high moral standards. He knew she would be the best kind of companion for his sister because she would caution Abigail about the scoundrels of the world. Jenny knew, first hand, and would impart to Abigail, that the rules were not arbitrary but were in place for good reason. Had

Jenny not made that one breach, she would not be in the situation she now found herself.

He trusted her with more than his sister's reputation. He trusted Jenny with Abigail's safety.

∞∞∞

"You must dismiss her at once," Letitia Mortimer declared. It was a bright, sunny morning unusual for early December, and Mortimer determined to spend it out of doors. He finished his paperwork while the grooms readied an open carriage for him. He was anxious to be on his way and was not in the mood for another altercation with his mother.

Jenny had been with them for four months and nearly every day of that time his mother had come to him with some complaint about her. She refused to yield in her dislike of Jenny Carlisle even though Abigail loved her. Perhaps that was enough reason for his mother to hate her. She was no longer the one Abigail looked to for advice or conversation.

"I am not going to dismiss her," he said. He stood and prepared to leave, but his mother would not be put off.

"Have you looked at her lately?"

"I look at her every day over the breakfast table and again at dinner." He found Jenny to be an attractive, articulate, pleasant dinner companion. She was modest without being sanctimonious, quiet without being dull. She had a quick wit and intelligence that he found to his liking. As much fault as his mother found with her, he could find none.

Mortimer freely admitted to himself that he was infatuated with Jenny Carlisle. Had he been in a position to offer her marriage, he would do so. But he would not burden her with a husband who, though he may love her, could not make love to her. She deserved a man for a husband, not a eunuch.

"You aren't looking at the right place. She is swelling with child. The girl's in a family way, Richard. She is an unsuitable companion for my daughter. I demand that you dismiss her immediately."

Mortimer felt like he'd been punched, but he didn't let it show. Jenny was pregnant. How long had she known? Why hadn't she come to him?

He could not ignore his mother's demand. While they led a quiet life at Fairleigh, it was bound to get out, and they would be condemned by their neighbors. For himself, he didn't care. But for Abigail's sake, he could not allow that to happen.

"I will speak with Miss Carlisle." Mortimer hated the self-satisfied smile his mother wore as he left the room.

∞∞∞

"Miss Carlisle, would you please come drive with me?" Jenny and Abigail were in the conservatory playing cards.

"I should love to, Captain. Abigail is positively trouncing me. Wait a moment while I get my cloak."

He studied her as she walked away. She was a bit fuller than she'd been before, but she'd been too thin when they'd met. Perhaps his mother was wrong and the extra fullness was merely the result of regular meals and lack of worry.

They rode out the main gate and proceeded down the road to take one of the cow trails through the fields. Mortimer carefully considered what he should say, uncomfortable with the topic he had to broach.

"Miss Carlisle, are you well?" Not terribly eloquent, but the best opening he could manage.

"Quite well, Captain." She turned away from him

when she answered. That was telling.

"My mother is concerned that you may be. . .in somewhat of a delicate condition." There, he'd said it.

Jenny didn't respond. She kept her face averted so he couldn't see her expression. Mortimer stopped the carriage and put on the brake.

She'd been hoping it wasn't true. If she didn't say it aloud, if she didn't admit it, it wouldn't be true. She'd known since her first week at Fairleigh when her courses, which had always been regular, didn't come. Still, she thought it was perhaps because she was overset by recent events. The months passed and she ignored the fact that she never bled. She ignored her constant fatigue, her growing appetite, and her swelling stomach.

She tried to conceal it, always wearing a shawl, keeping her arms crossed at her middle. But Mrs. Mortimer had noticed. Captain Mortimer's mother knew, and Jenny was mortified.

She was also very, very scared. He'd supported her refusal to marry Gerald Dawson, but surely now even Captain Mortimer would see it as folly and send her back to face her fate.

"Jenny," he said gently. "Are you with child?"

She turned to him, tears streaming down her cheeks, and she could see that now he knew, too.

"Ah, Jenny, I am so sorry." He drew her into his arms and she sobbed into his chest.

"I'm so ashamed, I didn't know how to tell you. I will of course leave at once."

"You'll do no such thing."

"I must. Dear Captain Mortimer, you've been so kind, but I have made quite a muddle of things. I am an unmarried woman in a family way. There is no hope for me now."

"What do you want to do?" he asked her as if she had

any choices left to her.

"I'm afraid that I must go crawling back home and hope my family will take me in. I will have to beg Mr. Dawson to marry me after all and apologize to him for my foolishness in refusing months ago. He did, after all, try to do the honorable thing." The words nearly choked her.

"There is nothing honorable about Gerald Dawson." Mortimer couldn't contain his anger. If he ever laid eyes on the man again, he would kill him. The man was unfit to live. "Allow me to offer you another option." The solution was so simple and clear it surprised him. "Will you marry me, Miss Carlisle?"

FIVE

Jenny looked aghast. Mortimer wasn't sure if he should feel offended.

"I cannot allow you to do that, Captain. I cannot allow you to tie yourself to someone who is carrying another man's child."

Mortimer almost retracted his offer. He knew he wasn't being fair, taking advantage of her desperation as he was. He hadn't asked her for her hand before because he had nothing to offer her. Now he did. He could give her his name and his protection. It wasn't much, but it was all he had. And any military strategist knew that one had to press one's advantage.

"Miss Carlisle, Jenny, may I be frank?"

She nodded.

Mortimer cleared his throat. It wasn't an easy admission, but he had to make it. Once she knew, it would make his proposal more palatable. She would see that she could give him something he could never otherwise hope to have. She would realize that he was getting the better part of the bargain. Knowing Jenny, she wouldn't consider what she'd be giving up, only what she could give him. "If we marry, the child you are carrying is the only child I can ever hope to have."

She blinked. She hadn't understood.

"My injury has made it impossible for me to father a child of my own," he explained further. "I am proposing a marriage of convenience only. You gain a father for your child. I get a child I can call my own."

"Even knowing whose child it is?"

"It is your child."

Jenny jumped down from the carriage and walked up the road a way. He didn't follow her, getting in and out of the carriage was too difficult. He allowed her the time she needed to work things through.

When she returned, she came to his side of the carriage and placed her hand on his thigh. When she looked up at him, he saw such anguish, reminding him of the expressions he'd seen on young men after their first battle. One should never know such horror.

"I don't want this child." She spoke passionately, angrily. The vehemence of her tone startled him. "I would rid myself of it if I could. I hate it." Her hand squeezed his thigh so hard, he was grateful it was not his injured leg that she treated so violently. "I can find nothing good in its existence. It will be a constant reminder, for the rest of my life, of what that animal did to me. I will never be able to escape the memory of that night, the horrifying feeling of being trapped, violated. I hate him and I hate his child. I have tried these past months to deny its existence, to pretend I didn't feel it growing inside me, like some kind of parasite eating away at my soul."

Mortimer wiped her tears with his thumb. He wanted to leap down to the ground and hold her, to ease her pain. But he was trapped by his bad leg, closer to being an invalid than he wanted to admit. So he remained perched on the seat of the carriage while she ranted below him.

"If you want this child, you may have it. I will take your offer. I will marry you. I will give you this child, just don't expect me to love it. Don't expect me to have anything to do with it."

Mortimer didn't have to consider his response.

"No. That is not acceptable. I grew up with a mother who despised me. I will not do that to any child. I will not do that to this child."

"Then we have no bargain." She walked around the back of the carriage and climbed in beside him. "I will return to my family."

"And will you marry Gerald Dawson?"

She gave a bitter laugh. "I should. I should marry him and make his life as miserable as he has made mine. But no, I don't think there is anything, even this, that would make me marry him. I will simply become a burden to my family, the scandalous daughter they hide away in the attic."

"And the child?"

"Dawson can have the child. I don't want it."

"And what if he denies it?"

"Then I will drown it."

He wanted to shake her, stop her from speaking such vitriol. This was not the woman he had come to know. The woman he had come to love. He didn't recognize the shrew who sat next to him looking wild-eyed and bordering on madness.

Mortimer released the brake and turned the carriage toward home. They rode back to the house in silence. Jenny sat stonily, eyes forward, showing no emotion at all. As if she had spent all her emotions back in the road.

When they pulled up in front of the door, she would have jumped down before the carriage had even stopped if he hadn't grabbed her arm and stopped her.

"I will take the child," he said in his officer's voice, which brooked no argument.

"You may have it. I only wish you could take it now." Jenny jumped from the carriage without waiting for assistance, as though she couldn't wait to escape.

Mortimer, to his embarrassment, required the assistance of the groom who came to lead the horses and carriage back to the stable. He dragged himself up the front steps, each step sending shooting pains up his leg. His mother waited for him in the front hallway.

"Well?" she said. He motioned her to join him in the library.

"I will write to her father and tell him we are sending her home." He hated saying it, hated more having to do it.

"Good." Letitia hesitated before leaving the room. "Richard. . ." She rarely used his given name. It made him pay attention. "It isn't your child, is it?"

Mortimer gave a disgusted snort. "No, Mother, it isn't my child."

"Well that's something anyway. I didn't think even you would stoop so low as to have your mistress living under the same roof as your impressionable younger sister."

"How flattering that you think so highly of me, Mother. Now, if you'll excuse me, I think I will retire to my room for the rest of the afternoon. Please have luncheon without me."

∞∞∞∞

Mortimer couldn't wait to get off his feet. He lay on his bed and assessed his physical condition. The leg was not healing. If anything, it was getting worse. The area around the wound still felt tender and warm to the touch. The pain travelled down his leg and up into his hip.

His body was rejecting the lead ball lodged in his thigh. It wanted the foreign object out.

For a moment, he could understand some of what Jenny Carlisle felt. He hadn't asked for this musket ball in his leg, would give anything to have it removed, to have his leg back to normal. He wanted to be able to walk without limping, to ride astride a horse, to dance at a ball.

None of that was going to happen. The doctors at the field hospital had told him there was no safe way to remove the ball. His only chance of survival was to leave it in and hope it didn't shift and cause further damage. They hadn't told him that living with it would be such agony.

Nelson checked in on him at lunchtime. Mortimer didn't feel like eating but accepted the healthy dose of brandy Nelson proffered.

"Nelson, when you visited Miss Carlisle's father in Bath, how did he seem to you? Did he seem willing to take her back?"

Nelson had given a cursory report upon his return, saying only that Mr. Carlisle was content to allow his daughter to remain at Fairleigh.

"You can't be thinking of sending her back."

Mortimer was unsurprised by Nelson's vehemence, since Nelson held a particular fondness for Jenny. He often commented on how kind and soft-spoken she was. Nelson sang Jenny's praises whenever he had the chance. She'd earned his respect by being gracious and friendly to everyone, regardless of station. To Nelson, Jenny was the definition of a true lady.

"She may need to rejoin her family."

"The old bastard won't take her," Nelson said. "He threw her out once, he'll do it again."

"That's what I feared." Mortimer rose and tested his leg. It felt a little better. He limped over to his writing desk. "Still, I must write to him and tell him she can no longer stay here." Wearily, Mortimer prepared his writing implements.

"Captain, if it's a husband she needs, I am volunteering for duty." Nelson snapped to attention as though he were still under Mortimer's command.

"What makes you think she's in need of a husband?" Mortimer wondered how far the story of Jenny's condition had spread.

"There's some speculation among the servants that Miss Carlisle may be breeding, sir. Don't worry, Captain, no one is saying anything disrespectful about her. I've set them straight—they know she's no loose woman."

Mortimer dismissed Nelson and set about writing to Mr. Carlisle, but the pen hovered over the paper, dripping ink like spots of blood.

How could he condemn Jenny to a life of ruin? How could he send her back to the man so willing to deliver her to her rapist?

He couldn't. Not when he wanted her for himself. With every fiber of his being, he wanted what Jenny had to offer. Not only herself, a woman he cared for deeply, but a child he could never hope to have.

Paper balled in his fist.

He would have to convince her that she could care for the child. Or convince himself that it wouldn't matter if she did.

Would it matter? He could be both father and mother to the babe. Abigail would be a doting aunt.

He'd protect it from his mother. And from its own mother if need be.

He considered the situation from every angle, the same way he considered maps and strategies before a battle.

Marriage was the best solution for Jenny. That much

was clear. But marriage to him? If he were less selfish, he would encourage Jenny to marry Nelson. Nelson may not have money or property, but he could at least satisfy Jenny in bed.

The very thought of Jenny in bed with Nelson, or anyone else for that matter, sent a stab of jealousy through him that rivaled the pain in his leg.

Jenny was hurting. She was a gentle, kindhearted person who had been betrayed by those who should have protected her. Dawson took advantage of her trust and innocence. Her father blamed her for causing a scandal that wasn't her fault.

Even he placed conditions on his offer to marry her. She had every right to feel resentment toward the babe growing in her womb. As much as he resented the lead ball lodged in his leg. How would he feel if someone demanded he love it and be happy for its presence?

He'd tell them to go to Hell.

He had to convince Jenny that marrying him—not Nelson and certainly not Dawson—was the best solution for everyone.

∞∞∞∞∞

Jenny sat in the window seat in her bedroom staring across the fields. She couldn't even cry she was so numb. How could she have spoken those things to Captain Mortimer? Bad enough that she thought them, but to speak them aloud. She expected a lightning bolt to come down from heaven and smite her. How he must hate her now.

As horrified as she was by her actions, she couldn't change them. She couldn't take back one word of what she'd said because it was all true.

She did hate this child, would end its life if she were

able to. And she hated herself for feeling this way. She was a horrible, horrible person, unfit to be a mother. Why, she'd be a worse mother than even Mrs. Mortimer.

Jenny smiled at the thought. Well, perhaps she wouldn't be quite that bad.

She rested her hand on her stomach and tried to imagine the life growing within. Was it a boy or a girl? Would it look like her, or, God forbid, like its father. She'd thought Gerald Dawson handsome enough once. Now, she could only see the blackness of his soul.

She felt a slight fluttering in her womb. It felt like butterflies flitting around inside. The baby moved.

For the first time, she thought of it as a baby and not some monstrous creature. A warm feeling spread through her.

Perhaps Captain Mortimer was right. Perhaps she could make this her child and ignore its unfortunate paternity. Captain Mortimer would make a fine father, she had no doubt about that. He'd proven to be a wonderful brother, and though Mrs. Mortimer would never admit it, an admirable son.

Jenny looked around the bedroom she'd called her own for the past four months. She'd added a few personal touches here and there. A watercolor Abigail had painted and given to her. The needlepoint she had recently started. A rocking chair she'd found in the attic and had been allowed to bring down.

Jenny couldn't bear the thought of leaving Fairleigh. She had come to love the house and its inhabitants, even, to some degree, Mrs. Mortimer, even though the older woman made it quite clear that she didn't want Jenny living there at all. Fairleigh had become her home. She loved Abigail almost as much as her own sister, Delia.

And she loved Captain Mortimer. She wanted nothing more than to marry him. But she hated that his offer was made out of necessity not desire, that he offered a marriage of convenience, not love. That he once again needed to rescue her from the situation that her own foolishness had precipitated. As he had rescued her the night at the inn and again when she had been driven out of Bath.

Jenny stood and crossed to the cheval glass near the wardrobe. Her figure showed only the slightest roundness, but she knew it would increase in the next few months. Soon it would be obvious to more than just the observant few. Would the household assume it was Captain Mortimer's child? If they married, would it be viewed as a love match? A romantic story of the lowly companion attracting the attention of the master of the house.

There was nothing romantic about her story.

But, it did not have to be all tragedy. Captain Mortimer could benefit from this baby. He would have a child to raise. A child to love.

And she would do her best to love it, too.

She would try to put her scandalous past behind her and make every effort to be a good wife to Captain Mortimer.

And if she never could care for this child as a mother should, she would at least make every effort to conceal her feelings. The babe would never know it wasn't loved and wanted. That, at least, she could promise to do.

∞∞∞∞

Mortimer was dressing for dinner when a knock sounded on his door. Expecting Nelson, he called for him to come in. To his surprise, instead of Nelson, Jenny stepped through the door and closed it behind her.

"I would like a private word, please, Captain," she

said, not venturing further into the room.

Mortimer hastily buttoned his shirt and turned away from her to tuck it in at his waist. "By all means, Miss Carlisle, I believe we have much still to discuss." He donned his jacket while he directed her to the seating arrangement facing the fireplace.

Instead of sitting, Jenny stood in front of the fire and held out her hands to the warmth of the flames.

"I have reconsidered your kind offer, Captain. I would be honored and privileged to marry you."

"Have you reconsidered how you feel about the child?" Though he had convinced himself earlier it didn't matter—he would marry her even if she still held the child in murderous contempt—he knew now it wasn't true. He wanted her to love this child. Their child. It would be theirs for all intents and purposes.

"I felt it move this afternoon." A wistful smile appeared on her face. "I find that I cannot remain unmoved by it."

"It is an innocent, Jenny. As innocent as you. It is here through no fault of its own."

"It is far more innocent than I. I hold myself responsible for my actions, Captain. Had I not given Mr. Dawson the opportunity to assault me, I would not now be in this predicament."

Mortimer closed the distance between them. He turned her away from the flames to look at her.

"Gerald Dawson would have taken an opportunity had you not presented him with one. He is a vicious, violent, selfish man. You did not deserve his treatment of you. You are innocent, Jenny. Please believe that."

Tears welled in her eyes. "I wish I could, Captain. I wish I could."

"Then at least believe it of the babe."

"That I can do. If there is any good to come out of

this situation, perhaps it is the babe. If I can give you a son. . ."

"Or a daughter." Mortimer smiled. "It will be all right Jenny. I think we will get on quite nicely together."

"Thank you, Captain, for once again rescuing me."

"I have no doubt, Miss Carlisle, that you would have managed to rescue yourself had I not been available."

Mortimer felt a twinge of guilt. He knew full well that she had other options. Nelson, for one. He wasn't being noble as she believed, but selfish.

He turned away, ashamed of the gratitude he saw in her eyes.

∞∞∞∞

They went down to dinner together. Abigail and Letitia were already seated at the table. His mother looked severely displeased to see that Jenny would be joining them. She would be even more displeased by his announcement.

"Miss Carlisle has agreed to marry me," he said without preamble.

"What! I thought she was leaving!" Letitia shrieked.

"Leaving? Whyever would she be leaving?" Abigail had been totally ignorant of the drama unfolding around her all afternoon.

"She's not leaving." Mortimer seated Jenny at her place then proceeded to his own at the head of the table.

Letitia stood so suddenly her chair fell over behind her.

"I will not sit at table with this hussy." She stormed off.

Abigail looked appalled by her mother's performance. "I think it's just grand that you and Richard are to be wed."

"Thank you, Abigail."

"And don't worry about Mother, she'll come around, you'll see. Now, shall we eat?" Mortimer waved over the footman who stood by the sideboard waiting to serve.

"Captain. . ."

"Really, Jenny, under the circumstances, don't you think it's time you called me Richard?"

Jenny blushed and stammered, "R-Richard, perhaps you should go speak to your mother. It was not fair of us to announce it this way."

"I'll speak to her after dinner."

"Does this mean Jenny won't be my companion anymore?" Abigail helped herself to the fish being proffered.

"It means I'll be better than your companion," Jenny assured her. "We'll be sisters."

"And soon you'll have a niece or nephew to coddle as well," Mortimer added.

Jenny blushed again.

"God willing, that is," he amended. Though how they were going to explain a four-month baby he didn't know.

Now that he knew of Jenny's condition, he couldn't understand how he had missed it. She had a maternal glow. She could deny all she wanted that she cared for the babe, but her body betrayed her. Her appetite was good, he noted as she refilled her plate from the platter the servant presented her.

She caught him looking at her, and looking guilty, pushed the platter away. Mortimer laughed. Abigail looked confused. Jenny blushed and smiled.

This was what he wanted, he realized. A home and family. Sharing secrets, communicating with just a look.

Fairleigh had never been a home to him. There had never been laughter at the dinner table. His father had been autocratic, ready to pounce on the slightest misstep.

His mother had picked and nagged and made him feel worthless. His brother Elliot delighted in getting him into trouble. Luckily for her, Abigail, still in the nursery, had been spared those blighted family gatherings.

His family would be happy. He and Jenny may be making a marriage of convenience, but it would be a good marriage. He loved her kindness. She had settled into his heart. He may not be able to be a husband to her in the bedroom, but he would be one to her in every other way.

He would do his best to chase the sadness from her eyes, the haunting memories from her mind. He would do his best to make her happy.

∞∞∞∞∞

Letitia had her rooms at the farthest end of the family wing. She'd converted three bedrooms to form her suite. One room was her sitting room where she penned her correspondence, forced Abigail to read to her for hours, and entertained the few visitors who ever called on her. Another room served as her dressing room. Though she rarely attended social functions, Letitia had a wardrobe suitable for any occasion. The final room was her bedchamber.

Which was where Mortimer found her, taken to her bed, sickened by the prospect of his marrying Jenny Carlisle.

"So the child is yours, isn't it? You've been carrying on with her under this very roof. I have never been so disappointed in you." Letitia spoke from beneath the pile of blankets under which she hid.

Mortimer loved his mother, always had. But he had learned long ago he could not please her.

"Mother, I've always disappointed you." He pulled a chair up close to the bed so he could get off his bad leg.

"I have not acted dishonorably with Jenny, and she has not acted dishonorably either. She was victimized by a man who wanted to marry her for her father's money. He forced himself on her so that she would be forced to marry him. But she refused to tie herself to so brutal a man, and for that I admire her. Unfortunately, he left her with child."

"She should have married him. Wouldn't be the first time a marriage had started with force. What woman ever gets to choose her husband? Do you think your father and I were a love match? But she's gotten what she wanted, didn't she? Instead of some penniless beggar, she gets a wealthy landowner. You may think you're saving her, Richard, but perhaps this is what she had planned all along."

"Perhaps it is." Mortimer refused to contradict her, giving her what she expected. In truth, she made a valid point. This could all be a scheme by an ambitious girl to snare herself a wealthy husband. But he didn't think so. He had become a good judge of character in his years in the military, and he judged Jenny's character to be sound.

His mother was right, though. Most women in Jenny's circumstance would have done what was expected of them and married the man. Yet, quiet, unassuming Jenny refused. She had a strength of will that he admired.

She would be a good partner to him.

"Regardless of her intentions, Mother, I am going to marry her. She will be your daughter-in-law, and I must ask, no, I must demand that you treat her with respect."

"And if I can't?" His mother sat up in bed and met his steely tone with one of her own.

"Then perhaps it is time you went to visit your relatives. You have some cousins in Yorkshire, I believe, don't you?"

"You would banish me from my own house?" she

sputtered.

"Need I remind you, Mother, that it is in fact my house now. You are, of course, welcome to live here with us." He paused before commanding, "As long as you treat Jenny with respect."

"You insolent, ungrateful whelp. Putting that harlot above me, your own mother."

"Shall I instruct your abigail to start packing your things, Mother?"

Like a good soldier, Letitia Mortimer knew the value of a strategic retreat.

"You will regret this, Richard. She will make your life a misery."

"It is my life, Mother."

"Just keep her away from me."

"Believe me, Mother, she will stay far away from you."

SIX

They were married in a small ceremony in Fairleigh's best drawing room. The groom's mother was noticeably absent as were any relations on the bride's side. Nelson stood witness for Mortimer, and Abigail played maid of honor for Jenny. The neighbors who had come for the nuptial feast could see from the way the couple looked at each other that it was a love match. After all that Captain Mortimer had been through, both at home and on the Peninsula, it was gratifying to see him find happiness with this charming young lady.

Only one awkward moment marred the ceremony. When the minister instructed Mortimer that he could kiss the bride, he leaned in for the kiss, but Jenny pulled away and cringed. Mortimer quickly recovered, lifting her hand to his lips instead and lightly kissing her palm.

∞∞∞∞

The festivities lasted well into the evening. Jenny was ready to drop she was so tired, but she waited for Captain Mortimer—Richard—to escort her to her room. Or his room.

He'd proposed a marriage of convenience, but she didn't know if he intended for them to share a bedroom. She didn't know if she wanted them to.

She loved Richard and was happy to be his wife. But when he'd tried to kiss her during the ceremony, she felt trapped, suffocated. It had lasted only a moment, but he'd noticed. She'd hurt him, she knew.

Her reaction appalled her. She vowed never to hurt him that way again, no matter what it cost her.

Finally, the last guests said their good-byes and Richard came to her. He held out his elbow for her to grasp and led her upstairs. He didn't turn left at the landing to take her to her own room, the room next to Abigail that she'd had since her arrival. He turned right and led her down the corridor toward his own room.

Jenny's heart fluttered in her chest. She didn't know what he would expect from her.

He stopped in front of a door.

"Your maid is waiting inside to ready you for bed. Sleep well, wife." He kissed her lightly on the forehead. This time, Jenny didn't freeze with fear.

The door opened from the inside and Jenny turned to greet Nellie, her maid. Richard continued along the corridor to the next door, which Jenny recognized as his room. Her room connected to his.

As she readied herself for bed, her eyes kept wandering to the door that led to Richard's room. Was it locked? Would he join her once the maid had left?

He said he was incapable of getting her with child, but would he make any other demands on her?

Nellie brushed out her hair to a bluish sheen. Jenny dismissed her and climbed into bed. It reminded her of the night she'd slept in Richard's room at the inn. She'd thought then that she'd be unable to sleep for fear of him barging in on her. Like that night, her fears were not enough to keep her from falling into a deep, dreamless sleep.

Jenny awoke in the middle of the night. Something had awakened her. A sound coming from the next room. A low moan that sounded almost primitive. She listened, trying to identify it. It wasn't an animal, at least, no animal that she recognized.

In the dark, the sound was eerie. Jenny had never been given to night fears, but tonight, sleeping in an unfamiliar bed, the curtains drawn across the windows to shut out even the merest glimmer of light, she felt afraid.

Without thinking, she leaped from the bed and ran toward the connecting door. To the one place she knew she would be safe. In Captain Mortimer's arms. Richard. Her husband.

Jenny turned the knob, relieved to find that the door was not locked from the other side. He hadn't locked her out.

His room glowed with moonlight streaming through the windows. Frigid air blew through her night rail, and she realized that the casement windows were cracked open. Hurrying across the cold floor, she approached the bed. She could see a mound under the blankets. Shivering, she wanted nothing more than to climb under those blankets herself.

But she hesitated. She didn't want to join him in his bed uninvited. And she wasn't sure she wouldn't panic as soon as she did.

The moan sounded again and Jenny realized it came from Richard.

"Richard." She called to him from the foot of the bed. "Richard, wake up please."

He stirred and sat up, fully awake in an instant.

"Jenny, what is it? What's wrong?"

"I heard something that frightened me."

He drew back the covers in welcome. "Come, come join me, you're shivering."

Jenny climbed into the bed beside him and he pulled the blankets over her, enveloping her into a haven of warmth. As his arms came around her, she felt safe, not threatened. This was Richard, her hero. Her protector.

"What did you hear? Do I need to charge in there and kill a mouse?"

"Very funny," she grumbled as she snuggled closer to him, trying to absorb the heat of his body. "I heard you moaning. You must have been dreaming."

He stilled beside her. "I'm sorry, I didn't mean to disturb you." His voice sounded cold and distant.

"Do you dream very often?"

"Every night. War leaves behind nightmares."

Mortimer shifted, trying to find a more comfortable position for his leg.

"I thought perhaps your leg pained you." Jenny was too observant, he realized.

"I don't know if it's the leg or the nightmares, but I rarely enjoy an uninterrupted night's sleep."

"I'm sorry I woke you. I'll return to my room." She started to leave, but he held her in place.

As soon as Mortimer realized what he was doing, he released her. Jenny lay still as a stone beside him.

"Please stay, Jenny." He wanted it to be her choice. Needed for her to know there was no coercion involved. He would not force her, would never force her to do anything she didn't choose to do.

"Why?" He heard the unmistakable suspicion in her tone.

"Jenny, I won't ravish you if that's what you fear. Even if that were my intent, I am not able to. But I would never hurt you. You have to trust me on that."

"I do trust you, Richard."

Mortimer's heart filled with some inexplicable emotion. Joy mingled with an intense satisfaction. Jenny trusted him. "Then stay with me. Sleep beside me, Jenny. Help keep the nightmares at bay."

"But your leg. What if I hurt it?"

"It's a chance I'm willing to take."

They settled themselves beneath the blankets, Jenny nestled against his side. They talked briefly about the day, the friends and neighbors who had come to wish them well. They avoided discussing her family or his mother. They laughed. Jenny giggled. Mortimer discovered he could make her hysterical by tickling the back of her knee.

Their conversation grew quieter and more infrequent. Mortimer waited until he heard her breathing grow deep and regular before drifting off himself. His last conscious thought was that Jenny Carlisle snored. He remained conscious long enough to correct himself. Jenny Mortimer snored.

∞∞∞∞

Christmas morning dawned icy cold but sunny with cloudless blue skies. Jenny dressed in the blue velvet dress Richard had given her. It was far too luxurious for a day spent at home with no one but family, but she wanted to wear it to please him.

The Mortimer family, including Letitia, who had decided that sulking in her room accomplished nothing, drove the short distance to the village church for Christmas morning service.

Three weeks married and already showing with child, Jenny thought as Richard helped her out of the carriage. What would the vicar think?

Once seated in the pew Richard leaned close to

whisper in her ear, "What are you smiling at?"

"Do you think the vicar is appalled by my condition?" she whispered back.

"I think he's impressed and wondering how I did it."

Jenny bit back a laugh.

Even though they had not consummated their marriage, she and Richard had spent every night of their married life together. In the dark quiet of the night, they had learned about each other. They shared the same uncommon sense of humor and often found themselves laughing over some incident that had occurred during the day. Richard told her he hadn't slept better in years. And because he was sleeping well, his leg seemed to pain him less during the day.

At least, that's what he told her. Jenny kept a cautious eye on him. When he seemed to be moving more stiffly, she called for a hot bath for him to soak in. When he couldn't hide his wince of pain, she brought brandy to soothe him. She tried to do it graciously so he barely noted the attentions. She was ever conscious not to hurt his pride.

When they returned to Fairleigh for the Christmas feast, a note awaited her.

"It's from Aunt Julia," she exclaimed. She'd written to her aunt about her marriage, had invited her to the wedding, but had received no reply. Jenny assumed that her father still forbade Julia to communicate with her. "Oh, Richard, she's been ill. She says she would have attended our wedding otherwise, no matter what my father threatened to do to her. She invites us to visit her in Bath for the New Year festivities."

"Then of course we shall go."

It would be their first venture into Bath Society since her ignominious departure from the city in late summer.

"Everyone will believe that what Dawson said was

true, you know. That you and I were lovers."

"Let them. It makes a wonderfully romantic story. You, betrothed to a man you cannot abide, learn that the man you truly love has returned from the Peninsula just in time to stop your wedding. Perhaps I kidnapped you from your bedroom that morning and carried you off to Bath. We were forced to spend the night at an inn because of foul weather. Your betrothed came after you, but was no match for true love." Mortimer stopped when he saw the look she gave him. He had become accustomed to her sharing his humor, but she did not look amused. She looked like he had struck her.

"Jenny, I'm sorry. That was callous and unthinking of me."

She tried to make light of it. "It's true, though. Everything you said. What a wonderfully romantic tale with which we can regale all of Society." Tears welled in her eyes, and she knew she had to excuse herself immediately before she released a sob and truly embarrassed herself.

"To hell with what Society thinks. Jenny, let them imagine what they will. We know the truth. We know you are blameless."

"I wish your romantic tale were true, Richard. You can't imagine how much I wish it were true."

∞∞∞∞

Mortimer readied the carriage with plenty of warm blankets and a coal scuttle to warm their feet. The last day of December dawned cold and crisp. A winter storm had passed through the day before bringing sleet and high winds that tore down branches. He would not have chosen this day to travel, but he would not disappoint Jenny. She was looking forward to her reunion with her aunt.

Bath was but a two-hour carriage ride away. Mortimer had every confidence in his driver, Oscar Dunlap, a local man who traversed the Bath road almost daily. There was no reason for him to feel so ill at ease. Still, he checked the harnesses himself before they set off.

Not wanting to alarm Jenny in any way, he put his uneasiness aside. Jenny had had Cook pack a midmorning picnic for them though they had both eaten heartily at breakfast. Mortimer knew that Jenny could not go two hours without demanding sustenance.

"The babe is always hungry," she said. He rested his hand on her now swollen belly and felt the baby kick. Mine, he thought. This child is mine.

They got underway just after nine, hoping to reach Julia's in time for the luncheon she had planned in their honor. The roads were bad, worse than Mortimer had anticipated. Oscar had to stop on several occasions so Mortimer and he could move branches out of the roadway.

They passed one unlucky traveler who had landed in a ditch and helped to pull the carriage back onto the road and reconnect the team so the hapless gentleman could continue on his way.

"It's no better up ahead," the gentleman warned them. "I'm heading home myself, decided not to continue on to Bath today."

"What do you want to do, Jenny?" Mortimer asked. They had been on the road for nearly three hours and were little more than half way.

"It seems that it would make little difference what we do," Jenny said. "Going back or going forward will take the same amount of time. Surely as we get closer to Bath the roads will be clearer?" Mortimer couldn't dismiss the hope in her voice. They decided to press on.

∞∞∞∞

Jenny had finished her picnic, which became their luncheon. The coals had lost any heat and her feet were frozen, but she wouldn't complain. Richard did his best to keep her entertained, and free from worrying, by regaling her with stories of his military career. They were carefully edited stories, she knew. Battles were fought without blood or violence, no one died in Richard's stories, and soldiers always acted nobly.

But from having spent the past three weeks listening to him talk in his sleep, she knew what war was really like. And she knew how much Richard needed to pretend that it wasn't.

The stories she liked best were the ones about what happened off the battlefield when the men were in encampments—the tricks the men played on each other, the courage of the officers' wives who followed the drum, the daily intrigues and romances of men far away from home.

Richard had just launched into another tale when they heard a horrible grinding sound and the carriage lurched to a halt, throwing both of them off their seats.

∞∞∞∞

Mortimer managed to catch Jenny before she went flying into the carriage wall—or worse, out the door which had popped open at her side. Before they had a chance to right themselves, the carriage lurched again. The horses screamed in panic and Oscar shouted at them to get out.

Mortimer tried to shift so he could lift Jenny out of the carriage, but his leg had been jolted and the pain nearly brought him to tears. He couldn't stand, the carriage was at an awkward angle, both he and Jenny were tangled in her skirts. If the danger hadn't been so great, they would have found the situation humorous.

"Hold tight," Oscar yelled. "I'm releasing the horses."

Jenny tried to pick herself up off the carriage floor and exit through the open door. Whether it was her movement or the sudden release of the horses, Mortimer didn't know, but the carriage toppled, somersaulted off the road, and crashed into a tree. Mortimer watched in horror as Jenny flew through the open door and landed with a thud on the ground several feet below.

The crash had caused the side of the carriage to cave in, wedging Mortimer's leg between it and the seat. He couldn't move.

"I'll get you out of there in just a moment, Captain," Oscar called from outside.

"Check on Mrs. Mortimer first, Oscar," Mortimer ordered.

"I'm fine, Richard. Let Oscar get you out." She didn't sound fine. Her voice was weak, and he could tell she was in some pain.

It seemed like hours before Oscar moved the seat enough to release Mortimer's leg. Of course his bad leg was the one trapped, luck would have it no other way, Mortimer thought with bitter irony.

Once freed from the carriage, Mortimer assessed the situation. Neither he nor Jenny were in any condition to walk. Jenny was pale and had a gash on her forehead. She tried to appear calm, but he could see she was shaken.

"Oscar, mount one of the horses and ride to the nearest house to get help," Mortimer commanded. He could not put any weight on his leg at all so he crawled to where Jenny sat leaning against a tree. The cold ground had her shivering.

Oscar brought them the blankets from inside the carriage, and they huddled together to keep warm.

Fortunately, the accident had occurred not far from a cottage and it wasn't long before Oscar returned with some men and a wagon to bring them to warmth and safety.

"The roads are treacherous today, just treacherous," Mrs. Carson, the woman of the house, opined as she got Jenny settled in a rocking chair by the fire. Jenny nodded, uncharacteristically quiet. Mortimer knew something was wrong but couldn't ask her in the crowded cottage great room.

"Is there a physician nearby that you could fetch?" Mortimer asked Mr. Carson.

"Not near enough, I'm afraid. Not on a day like this."

They had no other choice but to accept the Carson's hospitality and spend the night. And hope it warmed up enough tomorrow to make the roads passable again. Mortimer asked Oscar to help him move his chair next to Jenny.

"How are you feeling, Jenny?" he asked quietly when Oscar settled him next to her. He cursed his damned leg for making such an invalid of him. He wanted to lift her into his arms and hold her on his lap, but he had to content himself with patting her hand.

"I don't feel well, Richard." He could see the fear on her face.

SEVEN

Jenny had landed hard when she fell out of the carriage. She'd tumbled headfirst out the door but had managed to twist midair and land on her side. She could feel the bruises forming and every inch of her ached. But they were minor compared to what was happening inside.

She hadn't felt the baby move all afternoon. As she sat in the rocker in the Carson's kitchen, she kept her hand firmly pressed against her belly waiting for the slightest movement. Nothing came.

Now she felt moisture between her legs. She needed to use the privy, needed to check to see what leaked between her thighs, but she was afraid. As long as she sat and rocked and ignored what was happening to her body, she could still believe everything was fine. The baby would be all right.

But then a pain tore through her middle as though someone had sliced her open with a knife, and she cried out. Richard started issuing orders. Mrs. Carson rushed over and lay a blanket down on the floor and Oscar and Mr. Carson helped Richard, from his seated position, lower her to the floor.

Richard gasped and Jenny saw that blood drenched the seat of the chair she'd been sitting in.

"Oh, dear Lord, she's losing the babe," Mrs. Carson whispered. The woman sprang into action, issuing her own orders left and right, deftly taking command as the experienced midwife she was.

"You're in good hands," Mr. Carson said as he lifted Jenny in his strong workman's arms and carried her into the Carson's bedroom. "My wife attends all the births around here. She knows what to do."

Mrs. Carson shooed everyone out of the room and tended to Jenny.

"There, there, now, it'll be all right. I've lost two babies myself, I have." Mrs. Carson put a clean sheet under Jenny and bathed her thighs. Together they waited for the next pain to take over. They didn't have to wait long.

The contraction shook Jenny and she felt something gush between her legs.

"There's the little mite now," Mrs. Carson said gently. Reverently, the older woman wrapped it in toweling. Three contractions later, Jenny lay spent on the bed, panting and perspiring.

"Would you like to hold him?"

Him? It was a boy then? Mrs. Carson placed the tiny bundle in Jenny's arms. He was so small, barely two inches long, but he was fully formed. There were his fingers and toes and the almost imperceptible indication of his sex.

Jenny started to cry.

"I could have loved you," she whispered. "My poor baby, I would have loved you."

She had caused this. This was what she'd wanted, what she'd wished for. Everyone else might call it an accident, but she knew. And Richard knew. She had killed her baby. He was dead because she wanted him dead.

∞∞∞∞

Mortimer sat helplessly by the fire. His cane had been abandoned back in the carriage. Even with it, he doubted he could walk. His leg was numb. He had no control over it, couldn't move it more than a few inches. Every once in a while, it would spasm and shake and he couldn't make it stop.

The accident had crippled him.

Jenny needed him and he could not to go to her. Frustration made him curt and disagreeable. Oscar left the cottage to check on the horses, but more likely to get away from him.

Mr. Carson sat calmly at the table. The room had cleared at the sight of Jenny's blood. The neighbors who had come to their aid scurried home to their dinners.

"Please find out what's going on." Mortimer had tried raging, tried ordering, now he begged. He was ready to crawl across the kitchen floor to get to the bedroom door. Jenny had stopped screaming and the house was enveloped in a deafening silence.

Mrs. Carson opened the door.

"The babe's gone, Mr. Mortimer. I'm sorry. Owen, help Mr. Mortimer in to see his wife."

Obediently, Owen Carson half carried Mortimer into the room. Mrs. Carson pulled a chair up next to the bed. Jenny was holding a bundle in her arms.

"I'm so sorry, Richard."

He'd never seen anyone look so bleak.

"I killed your son."

"Shh, shh, Jenny," he said, taking the bundle from her arms and seeing the pathetic creature nestled within. "It wasn't your fault. It was my fault. I knew the roads were bad, I should not have let you come. Please don't blame yourself."

"Don't you understand, Richard? This is what I wanted, what I wished for. God is merely granting me what I begged Him for. I'm so sorry."

She cried huge, aching sobs that seemed to come from the very heart of her.

"I'm so sorry," she kept repeating, over and over again.

"Jenny," he said sharply, trying to jolt her out of her hysteria. "We will discuss this later. Now, I want you to rest. We'll return to Fairleigh in the morning."

His firm tone had the desired effect, for she discontinued her mantra and gave him a sober look.

"I won't be returning to Fairleigh with you, Richard. There's no reason for us to remain married now that the baby is dead. I will go live with Aunt Julia."

Not wanting to have this discussion when she was obviously overwrought, he said, "We'll discuss that in the morning, too, Jenny. Now, please rest."

She settled herself down in the bed.

"Where will you sleep, Richard?"

"Right here next to you, Jenny. Go to sleep now."

Exhausted from her ordeal, Jenny did as he said and allowed sleep to take her.

∞∞∞∞∞

They didn't discuss it in the morning, or on any morning that followed. Jenny didn't mention leaving again and Richard didn't bring it up. She never spoke about the baby. They went about their life together much as they had before the accident with one exception. Jenny no longer joined him in his bed at night.

Richard didn't invite her either. His leg had been

damaged further in the accident, and he was restless at night, often not sleeping at all.

Jenny was subdued but otherwise apparently fully recovered. She continued to act as companion to Abigail and tried not to let her sorrow show. It took great effort to present a calm demeanor when she raged inside. She felt like a gifted actress so adept did she become at pasting on a smile when Abigail said something amusing. Sometimes, she even managed an almost natural sounding laugh.

A performance worthy of Drury Lane.

Each night she crawled into her bed utterly spent from the effort of keeping up the pretense that all was as it should be.

The only person she didn't try to pretend in front of was Richard. He, she simply avoided. They were polite to each other when they encountered one another in a hallway. At dinner each evening, they were especially courteous. Richard was always solicitous of her health and well being and she dutifully inquired after his.

Richard had brought their son home and had him buried in the family plot. He'd put up a stone that said "Baby Mortimer." Jenny visited it every afternoon when Abigail spent her prescribed hour reading to her mother.

∞∞∞∞

Mortimer wasn't fooled by Jenny's performance. He knew she was unhappy. The loss of the baby had upset her. As much as he wanted to comfort her, he knew he could not give her the one thing she needed most. Everyone knew that the best cure after such a loss was to have another child. With him, Jenny could never hope to have another child.

He watched her from his bedroom window as she

made her way again to the small plot where he'd buried her child. Mortimer knew grief, having experienced it many times on the Peninsula. Men lost their best friends in battle. As an officer, he'd witnessed the grieving process on many occasions, the initial sorrow that became anger followed by acceptance. But Jenny's grief did not follow the natural course he expected. She seemed unable to move beyond sorrow. It was a palpable thing, her sorrow, a heavy burden that seemed to weigh down her fragile frame.

He couldn't continue to watch her fade away without doing something to save her. He needed to rescue Jenny once again.

"Nelson, please go and ask Mrs. Mortimer to come see me. She's visiting the grave."

Mortimer hated not being able to go to her himself, but his leg did not allow him to go traipsing across the fields. Since the accident, it was all he could manage to make it down the stairs twice a day. Nelson helped him down in the morning for breakfast, after which he spent a few hours in his study going over accounts and hearing reports from Mr. Godfrey, the steward. He took his lunch in his room. By then, he needed to lie down and stretch the cursed thing out.

He forced himself to dress for dinner each evening and once again Nelson assisted him to the dining room. Mortimer was putting on a performance as well. He pretended that his leg didn't pain him constantly, that he could actually carry on a conversation when all he really thought about was how much it hurt and how soon he could rest it again.

He'd allowed Jenny to drift alone for three weeks because he was caught up in his own tragedy.

He knew he was going to lose his leg.

∞∞∞∞

The biting January wind tore through Jenny's cloak, but she didn't feel it. She didn't feel anything these days. She was numb inside. She stood looking down at the flat stone marker and couldn't even feel guilt anymore. She walked in a fog, devoid of joy, devoid of pain, feeling nothing.

An improvement, she supposed, over the rage she'd felt those first few days after the accident. She had finally let the baby into her heart, had finally accepted it, him, as her own. What kind of God would play such a trick on her, letting her hope for a bright future then snatch it away? Only a cruel God. She'd raged at Him and at the universe, but mostly she raged at herself. What kind of despicable person wished for her own child to die?

She should have felt relief at not having to bear Dawson's son. But all she felt was sorrow.

Someone came up behind her—she heard the crunch of footsteps on the frosty grass. She didn't turn around.

"Mrs. Mortimer," Nelson called from a respectful distance.

Jenny turned away from the grave marker and faced him.

"The captain would like you to come see him now."

Without saying a word, she walked back toward the house.

"Mrs. Mortimer," Nelson said as he got into step beside her. "Please convince the captain to see a doctor. His leg's been hurting him awful since the accident, but he won't let me call anyone to come look at it."

Jenny stilled Nelson with a touch to his arm, and they stopped a few feet from the house.

"Captain Mortimer is hurt?" Why hadn't she noticed? But she knew why. She'd been too caught up in her own misery to notice anyone else's.

"Yes ma'am," Nelson said. "The leg got twisted in the carriage and it's worse than ever. He won't see a doctor because he's afraid the man will want to saw it off."

Jenny blanched. The thought of Richard losing his leg shook her deeply. He was such a proud man, capable and strong. He would not take the loss lightly. No, he would not take the loss well at all.

It was time for Jenny to rescue the captain.

∞∞∞∞

She brought in the cold, fresh air. Mortimer could smell the outdoors on her cloak, which she hadn't taken the time to remove before rushing up to see him. He wondered what Nelson had told her to get her here so fast. She looked concerned. For him. He was lying on his bed and would have gotten up to greet her, but she didn't give him a chance as she came in so quickly and plopped herself on the side of the bed next to him.

Taking his hand, she said, "Richard, I am so sorry. You've been ill and I have been selfishly wallowing in my own grief."

"You needed time to grieve, Jenny, I didn't want to disturb you with my ailments."

Jenny couldn't believe how pale he looked. How could she have been so blind? Tears sprang to her eyes. "Foolish man. Now, what's this I hear about you not wanting Nelson to fetch a doctor? I'm afraid I really must insist that you have a physician look at you."

His lips turned up in the hint of a smile. "You insist, do you?"

"As your wife, it is my responsibility to see you well cared for, especially when you are obviously incapable of caring for yourself. The accident must have caused a degeneration of your mental faculties or you would surely have called for a physician yourself."

"I'm not sure, woman, but I believe you just insulted me."

Jenny smiled down on him. "I would never insult you, sir. I am merely pointing out that you are not making the best judgments at the moment. Now, shall I have Nelson bring the doctor to you?"

He hadn't realized Jenny could be so bossy. This was the most life she'd shown since she'd lost the baby. If nursing him back to health would alleviate her sorrow, he would subject himself to the ministrations of a physician. It was past time, anyhow, he knew. He'd hoped the leg would heal on its own, but three weeks had passed and there was no improvement. If anything, it was getting worse, not better.

"Very well, Mrs. Mortimer. Since you insist, Nelson may fetch the doctor."

Nelson was out the door before he'd even finished the sentence.

"Now, sir, what was it you wanted to see me about?"

Mortimer wasn't sure he wanted to broach the subject now that she seemed to be back from the dark place she'd retreated to, but he felt he owed it to her.

Charging ahead, he said, "Jenny, our marriage was one of convenience, to give a name to the child and protect you from scandal. With the baby gone, you don't need my name and protection any longer." He cleared his throat so he could continue. "You'll want to have another child someday. You should have another child. And that's something I can't give you."

He'd thought of little else the past weeks as he lay abed each afternoon. He should never have married her in the first place, unable as he was to make love to her. Somehow, he'd convinced himself the child would make up for their lack of intimacy, the child would be enough. They'd be a family.

But now, with the child gone, he had to set her free. He'd allowed his selfishness to manipulate her into marrying him, but he loved her too much to force her to stay married to him.

Jenny looked stricken by what he said. "You want to send me away," she stated flatly.

"I want to give you the choice. You don't have to stay married to me. I won't force it on you."

Clenching her fists as if she wanted to hit him, she stood up to keep herself from doing so. All the grief and rage she had been keeping inside for the past three weeks burst out of her.

"Oh, very nicely said, Captain," she shouted at him in a tone filled with scorn. "I can't deliver what I promised so you'll set me aside. The only reason you married me was so you could claim my son as your own. Now he's gone, so you want nothing more to do with me. Very well, Richard, if that's what you want, divorce me."

Mortimer couldn't believe how he'd blundered. She didn't understand at all, was taking what he said and twisting it ways he hadn't even thought.

"There's no reason for a divorce, Jenny. We could have the marriage annulled since it was never consummated. If that's what you want."

"What I want? Since when has any man ever considered what I want? Gerald Dawson certainly didn't, my father certainly didn't. Now you. All you do is take what you want, and when I have nothing left to give you cast me aside. You don't give a damn about what I want."

He'd never heard Jenny curse before, hadn't realized she even knew how. He was angry now, too. Angry because he couldn't grab her and hold her in his arms and shake her if he had to, but more likely crush her in an embrace. Angry because he was an invalid and he would not saddle her with an impotent husband with only one leg. Couldn't she see that he was trying to do what was best for her?

"Do you really want an invalid for a husband? A man who is incapable of making love to you? A man who can never give you another child? Is that what you want, Jenny?" He was shouting now, too.

"Yes!" she yelled right back at him. The word rang in the room and stunned them both into silence.

"Why?" Mortimer whispered after a few heartbeats.

"Oh, Richard, don't you know? Because I love you. Because you were willing to take me at my worst. Now, Richard, tell me. What do you want? I will honor your wishes. If you want to set our marriage aside because you hope to marry for love someday, I will not fight you. But if it is from some misguided sense of nobility, I will not allow it."

"You have become rather shrewish today, Mrs. Mortimer."

Jenny ignored the insult. "Do you want to end this marriage?" she asked again.

He beckoned her to him. Pulling her down on the bed beside him, he nestled her in his arms. "I want you to be happy, Jenny. Do you really believe you will be happy if you stay with me?"

"I think the only chance I have of happiness is with you." Jenny lightly stroked his cheek, ran her fingers over his mustache, and as they brushed his lips, lingered for his kiss. "The fact that you cannot make love to me is one of the reasons I want to stay married to you. I am not sure that I could willingly accept your attentions should you force them on me."

He wanted complete honesty from her. If they were to make their marriage a real marriage and not merely one of

convenience, she had to tell him how she really felt. But hearing her say the words felt like a punch to the stomach. She wanted to stay married to him because he was impotent? Did she find him so repugnant that she couldn't bear the thought of making love to him? As soon as he thought it, he realized the truth.

"Jenny, surely in time, the memory of what Dawson did to you will fade. You will find yourself wanting to have a child, to share the intimacies of marriage with your husband."

"I cannot bear the thought of any man ever impaling me that way again. No man. Not even you." She raised herself on her elbow so she could see his eyes. "Can you accept that?"

"I don't know," he said honestly. "But I can tell you this. I cannot bear the thought of any man other than me lying with you. Ever."

Jenny leaned down and lightly kissed his mouth. "Then it appears, Captain, we are to remain wed."

"I hope you don't regret it, Jenny."

"I hope that you don't, either."

EIGHT

Doctor Garvey came from Bath early the next morning. He examined Mortimer's leg in a cool, professional manner, issuing orders like "move it this way" and "lift it up" as he did so. He "hmmph'd" and "hmm'd," but said not a word to reassure Mortimer that the leg could be saved.

"Tell me the truth, Doctor," Mortimer said when he could take the man's silence no longer. "Does it have to come off?"

"Won't do you any good to take it off," Doctor Garvey replied without preamble. "The ball's too high up. They'd have to cut it off at the joint and your chances of surviving that would not be very good. No, I think the only solution is to get the ball out."

"The doctors at the field hospital said it was impossible to remove it without me bleeding to death."

"Well, there's a surgeon in London I know of whom you might want to have a look. Mr. Michael Carmody. If anyone can get the ball out, he can."

Doctor Garvey left him a bottle of laudanum for the pain and advised him to stay off the leg, which Mortimer had realized on his own.

Mortimer should have felt relieved that Doctor Garvey didn't want to cut off his leg. Yet, he felt oddly disappointed. At least if the leg came off, there was a chance he would be free of the blasted, constant, searing pain. Doctor Garvey thought the ball might have shifted in the accident and now leaned on a nerve, which explained why he was in so much more pain. He had no explanation for the lack of control and muscle spasms. "Just the way the body reacts to a foreign object," was the only answer he could give.

Mortimer tried to put the best face on Doctor Garvey's prognosis as he could.

"At least the leg doesn't need amputating," he told Jenny after she had seen the doctor on his way. "And there's a specialist in London Doctor Garvey suggested I see. Mr. Carmody might be able to get the musket ball out."

"Then we must go to London at once," Jenny said.

"Perhaps we should write to Mr. Carmody first, Jenny. He may not be able to see me."

Jenny dispatched a letter right away, but a month passed before they received a reply. Apparently, the surgeon had been traveling in Scotland.

"He says he'll be able to see you on the ninth of April. Why, that's another month away! I think we should go and park ourselves on his doorstep and demand that he see you immediately." Jenny's indignation on his behalf gratified him, but Mortimer was in no hurry to see the surgeon. Though tired of being bedridden, and even more weary of the nearly constant, often excruciating pain he feared that if he saw Mr. Carmody and the man could not help him, he would have nothing more to hope for. He would be forced to accept that he would have to live like this for the rest of his life.

He wasn't sure how long he could go on, knowing there would be no chance of relief.

Putting off his visit another month would put off the inevitable. Because in his heart, Mortimer didn't believe Carmody would be able to help him. He'd seen too many men die in field hospitals. He knew the dangers of surgery—the risks of infection, of bleeding, of bumbling physicians. Even if Mr. Carmody offered to surgically remove the lead ball, Mortimer wasn't at all sure he had the courage to go through with it.

As long as his visit to Carmody remained in the future, he could live in this limbo where he had hope the man could help him but had no decision to make about whether to let him try.

Mortimer knew Jenny was anxious about him. Since Doctor Garvey's visit, she had returned to his bed. She knew how restless he was at night. He'd suggested she return to her own room so he wouldn't disturb her sleep, but she had refused to go on her own account.

"Does having me here bother you?" she said, ready to take herself off if she made his rest uncomfortable. He couldn't lie to her. Having her sleep with him was the only thing that made the nights tolerable. He slept better with her head on the pillow next to his, the soft sound of her snoring lulling him like a lullaby.

Mortimer remained abed most of the time. Once he found a comfortable position, he was afraid to move for fear of a resurgence of pain.

Jenny made sure he was well cared for, often against his own objections. Nelson followed her orders now rather than his own. If it were up to him, Nelson would not shave him every morning nor would he have to put up with the torture of a daily bath, but Jenny insisted and Nelson, the traitor, listened to her.

Jenny also made sure he kept abreast of the household

accounts and had Mr. Godfrey report to him every afternoon, often waking him from a much needed nap for him to do so.

There were days when he wanted to strangle the woman. Why could she not let him be, wallowing in misery? But no, she drew back the curtains every morning to flood his room with sunlight even though he would rather it remain dark. She joined him in his room for his meals even though she should have been eating in the dining room with Abigail and Letitia. Why, she had even managed to get his mother to come visit him at least once a week. And whatever she had done that had also gotten her to concede he "might have done worse" than marrying Jenny, he'd never know.

Jenny did not allow him to feel like an invalid. She insisted that he perform his duties and not shirk his responsibilities.

He loved her more every day.

"We will go to London at the beginning of April. Do you think you can manage to find us a house to let for the Season?" he had said when she finished reading the letter from Mr. Carmody. "We may as well combine my visit to the surgeon with Abigail's first Season."

Jenny grew very still. "She's much too young still," she replied after taking a moment to collect herself.

"She turns eighteen next month," Mortimer replied reasonably.

"Richard, it would be better if we waited until next year for her come out. You'll be walking then and will be able to lead her on the dance floor."

"Jenny. . ." He opened his mouth to remind her once again that she shouldn't get her hopes up, that the chances were good that Carmody would be unable to help him, that he may never be able to walk—let alone dance—again.

She interrupted him. "It's too soon. My scandal will taint her. She won't be accepted. Richard, we have to wait." Clearly agitated, Jenny puttered about the room, folding a blanket at the foot of the bed and straightening the knick-knacks that decorated the mantel. Clenching a porcelain dog in her hand, she said quietly, "I want no part of a London Season, particularly if you would not be at my side." Abandoning the canine statue, she held out her hands toward him. "Look at me. I shake like a coward at the thought of facing London Society alone. My scandal is still fresh in everyone's mind—it was just last Season that I ran away on my wedding day only to marry someone else a short few months later. I don't know how many people know about the baby, but you know how gossip travels."

He knew she was right, but he also feared that if he didn't get Abigail launched this year, he may not be able to do it next year. If Mr. Carmody could not help him, he may not survive another year.

But he couldn't tell Jenny that.

"We don't know how long we'll need to be in London, assuming Mr. Carmody can treat me. You and Abigail should be able to enjoy some entertainments while I am under the doctor's care."

"As you say, we may be there only a short time. Why go to all the expense of leasing a house for the entire Season? Abigail and Letitia can stay here, there's no reason for them to come up to London with us. Really, Richard, this is not the right time to launch Abigail into Society."

Admitting defeat, Mortimer conceded.

"We will still need a place to stay while in London," he said.

"I'll write to my father and ask if we can use his London house. He is rarely in Town."

Mortimer knew how much it would cost her to make the request. He hoped it would provide an opportunity for Jenny and her father to mend the breach between them. She would need her family if his visit to Mr. Carmody failed.

Jenny's father graciously allowed them to use his London Town house, an imposing edifice on the edge of Mayfair, for the month of April.

"You must vacate by the first of May," his letter said, "because your sister Delia will be starting her second Season and I want her free of your corrupting influence."

Jenny was disappointed that she would not be allowed to see her sister. It angered her that her father thought of her as a corrupting influence. How she wanted to tell him exactly what he could do with his Town house. But, for Richard's sake, she wrote him back accepting his kind offer.

Letitia insisted on going to London with them so that she and Abigail could visit the shops. Jenny argued that the trip was to improve Richard's health, not a shopping expedition. In the end, she reluctantly relented, but made it clear they would not be accepting any invitations, should they receive any, though she doubted any would be forthcoming. Given her tattered reputation and Letitia's long absence from Town, Jenny felt fairly certain the Mortimer family's stay in London would be largely unremarked upon

She couldn't have been more wrong.

They arrived in London late in the afternoon of April fourth. Jenny had wanted to arrive early to give Richard time to recover from the trip before seeing the surgeon. Two mornings later, a small announcement appeared in the London Times.

"Noted war hero arrives in Town. Captain Richard Mortimer, hero of numerous battles on the Peninsula, arrived in London late Tuesday. Accompanied by his wife, the former Miss Jenny Carlisle, and his mother, Mrs. Letitia Mortimer, as well as his young sister, Miss Abigail Mortimer, the captain and his family are in residence in the home of Mr. Douglas Carlisle, the captain's father-in-law."

"Oh, dear," Jenny said when she saw it. There would be no avoiding callers now. Not only would curiosity seekers be coming to see what kind of match a woman of her notorious past had made, they would be coming to worship a war hero. Jenny couldn't imagine how such a notice had gotten into the paper.

She had only to look at Letitia's satisfied smile to know.

"You sent this announcement to the Times?" Jenny was incredulous. Didn't Letitia understand they were here for Richard, not for their own enjoyment?

"And they printed it word for word. What an opportunity for Abigail, to be associated with a war hero."

"Haven't you heard a thing I said about this not being the right Season to launch Abigail?" Jenny had thought she and Letitia had reached an understanding of sorts. They were by no means friends, but Letitia had at least softened a bit. She seemed genuinely concerned about Richard's well being and seemed to want a good match for Abigail.

Now it appeared that the woman was purposely sabotaging her daughter's chances of a successful first Season.

"Yes, yes, you're all concerned about your scandalous past. Well, let me tell you something, no one cares about you. Richard's heroics far outshine any petty scandal you may have involved yourself in. You simply are not that important."

"You mean you're actually proud of your son?" Jenny wanted her to admit it. Letitia had never said one word to Richard even hinting she respected him for his heroics in the Peninsula war.

"I still think it was pure folly for him to retain his commission after his brother Elliot died, putting himself in danger as he did. Why, we wouldn't need to be here now if not for the injury he sustained well after the time he should have returned home and taken up his rightful place at Fairleigh. But, if Abigail and I can benefit from his cachet, so be it."

"You are a remarkable woman, Mrs. Mortimer," Jenny said in wonderment. The woman had a knack for turning every situation to her own advantage. Jenny hoped that Letitia was right this time and that the previous year's scandal did not reflect badly on Abigail.

If only her father would have some of Letitia's confidence. He, it seemed, was convinced Jenny's mere presence was enough to taint her sister Delia. Corrupting influence, indeed.

∞∞∞∞

Jenny guarded Richard against having to entertain unwanted callers, but at his insistence always welcomed fellow officers and subordinates from his military career. Most afternoons, their drawing room resembled a barracks with discharged men and commissioned officers sipping brandies and reminiscing.

Jenny saw a side of her husband she had not known. He had always been a hero to her, but she hadn't realized how many other lives he had saved. Richard did not speak willingly of his days at war. Though he laughed and traded tales with his comrades, it took a toll on him. Whenever their guests left, Jenny sensed a darkness in Richard that he tried to conceal.

More than one man who came to their door missed a limb, an arm or leg—others had lost an eye or wore scars on their faces. Most were soldiers who had been discharged because of their injuries. Many a man left after a visit to their house with banknotes in his pocket he hadn't had when he arrived.

Jenny admired Richard's generosity and his compassion. Seeing the plight of so many who had suffered injuries similar to, and, in many cases, worse than his own, seemed to strengthen his resolve. As the day of his visit to Mr. Carmody drew nearer, Richard grew determined to get well, vowing to submit to whatever treatment Carmody wanted to subject him to if it meant he would be whole again.

Jenny prayed he would not be disappointed.

∞∞∞∞

Mr. Carmody's surgery occupied the third floor in an unimposing building on Fleet Street. The surgeon himself was a gruff, scruffy, bearded man with absolutely no bedside manner. Mortimer liked him immediately.

Both he and Nelson were sweating by the time they reached the third floor landing with Nelson almost carrying Mortimer the whole way.

"Going down, I do it on my bottom," Mortimer said. Nelson, still catching his breath, simply nodded in agreement.

Mortimer was glad he had insisted Jenny stay at home. It would have insulted his dignity to have her see him like this, sweating with the exertion of getting up the stairs, each step an agony.

Mr. Carmody showed no sympathy for the two men as he ushered them into his consulting room.

"You've a musket ball lodged in your upper thigh that is causing you unbearable pain, is that correct?" Carmody didn't waste any time with niceties, but got right to the point. He had Mortimer lower his breaches and, with Nelson's help, sit on the examining table.

It took all of Mortimer's fortitude not to cry out as the doctor poked and prodded at the site of his injury. The tissue around the wound had thickened and scarred, but the area that radiated out around it was red and sensitive.

"The lead is causing blood poisoning. Only a matter of time before it kills you. I recommend removal. I can perform the operation tomorrow morning at London Hospital."

"What are my chances of surviving the surgery?"

"Better than your chances of surviving without it."

"Doctor Garvey said that removing the leg would kill me."

"I'm not removing the leg, just the musket ball."

"The surgeons in the field hospital said if they attempted it, I would bleed to death."

"London Hospital is a bit better equipped than a field hospital, Captain. You should have come to see me as soon as you got home."

Mortimer felt a mixture of elation and frustration, fear mingled with hope. The examination was over in less time than it had taken him and Nelson to climb the stairs.

"Too bad about that," Carmody noted as he helped Nelson position Mortimer so he could slide down the staircase in a most undignified manner. "I could have made a house call."

∞∞∞∞

Jenny would not be excluded from the visit to London Hospital. She, Nelson, and Mortimer arrived at the appointed time. Mr. Carmody was already there and took Mortimer into the surgical room. Jenny and Nelson were left to pace outside in the hallway.

Two hours later, Mr. Carmody came out to talk to them. Jenny almost fainted when she saw the blood covering the white apron he had donned for the surgery.

"Tell me he isn't dead," she said.

"He isn't dead," Carmody assured her. "Actually, things went well. He's sleeping now. I gave him opium for the pain. He'll need rest for at least a week, watch for signs of infection and putrefaction. I'll come see him later in the week."

And just like that, he was gone. With Nelson's help, Jenny commandeered two burly men to carry Richard out on a litter. He was awake and every time they jostled him, he winced with pain, but he remained stoically silent. They hired a wagon to carry him home. Then, Jenny sat vigil in her husband's bedroom in her father's house.

The fever came in the middle of the night. He'd been sleeping restfully for a few hours and Jenny had finally allowed herself to lie down beside him, being careful not to shift or move in any way that would irritate his healing leg. She must have fallen asleep because his thrashing jolted her awake. She had to call Nelson to help hold him still so he would not tear out Mr. Carmody's carefully sewn stitches.

Jenny bathed Richard's brow with cool water and spoke soothing words to him all through the night.

She could not lose him. Not now, not so soon after losing the baby. Not now when she knew that it was this man with whom she wanted to spend the rest of her life.

"Don't you dare die on me, Captain Mortimer," she ordered him as dawn lightened the room and his fever

spiked even higher. "I will not have it."

As though he heard her, Richard moaned, "No, no!" and started thrashing about again.

"Shh, shh, love," Jenny crooned. The sound of her soft, gentle assurances seemed to soothe him.

As soon as morning arrived, Jenny sent Nelson to fetch Mr. Carmody. The doctor would answer to her if Richard died of fever and infection. While Carmody examined Richard, Jenny left for her own room to wash and change her clothes, which were wrinkled and soiled from her nursing duties.

"How is he?" Letitia accosted her in the hallway.

Unable to ignore the real look of concern on the older woman's face, Jenny invited Letitia to keep her company while she changed.

"His fever spiked during the night," she said. "But Mr. Carmody is with him now. I have every confidence that Richard will recover and be well and whole again."

"I've lost a husband and one son. I don't want to lose another," Letitia said. "He thinks I favored Elliot over him and perhaps he's right. It was wrong of me. Richard had a knack for riling his father into a temper, and I nagged him to try to keep peace in the family. I should have defended him more, I know. But I will never forgive him for staying in that blasted inferno when Elliot died. He should have come home. He should have come home and none of this would have happened." Letitia sobbed softly and Jenny went to her and hugged her. In her own, selfish way, Letitia loved Richard, too.

"He's going to be fine. Now, let's go down to breakfast before Abigail eats it all."

In a fresh gown, Jenny felt more confident and assured. Richard was a soldier, he would not give up without a fight.

Mr. Carmody sipped a cup of tea at the dining room

table when Jenny and Letitia arrived. Before him sat a plate piled with everything the sideboard offered—rashers of bacon, black and white pudding, fresh eggs, toasted bread, a great slab of ham. Jenny didn't attempt to keep the irritation out of her voice as she asked, "How is my husband, sir?"

"Much as I expected, Mrs. Mortimer," Mr. Carmody answered around the eggs he'd just shoved into his mouth. "His fever is a good sign—his body is fighting off infection. The surgical site is clean and clear. I replaced the bandaging and left instructions with his man, Nelson." The doctor waved his fork, precariously piled with egg and pudding, over his plate. "Since you called me needlessly, I figured you owed me breakfast."

Jenny was about to tell him what he could do with his breakfast when Abigail jumped into the breach.

"I do hope he's well enough to go to the Ashfords' ball.".

NINE

"Ball?" Jenny looked accusingly at Letitia.

"Cornelia Ashford is a very dear, very old friend of mine," Letitia said without apology. "It would have been rude to refuse her."

"And just when is this ball?" Jenny hated having this conversation in front of the supercilious physician, but she couldn't contain herself. She hadn't known that Letitia even had any old and dear friends. The woman was determined to launch Abigail this year whether in Abigail's best interests or not. How did she think the girl would fare at her first ball without Richard there to escort her?

"The last week in May, I believe," Letitia averred.

"The twenty-fifth of May," Abigail answered at the same time.

"Well, we are returning to Fairleigh at the end of April, so you'll have to send your regrets."

"I wouldn't recommend Captain Mortimer traveling that soon, Mrs. Mortimer," Carmody piped in. Jenny caught the wink and smile he directed at Abigail. "The first of June is soon enough for him to travel."

Letitia gave Jenny a sly smile. "Perhaps you'd best write your father and apprise him of the situation."

Jenny turned and left the room without eating. She needed to get away from the lot of them.

Richard rested quietly when she returned to him. Nelson stood guard as she'd expected.

"He's very lucky to have such a friend as you," she said.

"He's lucky to have found a wife such as you, Mrs. Mortimer," Nelson returned the compliment.

Jenny shook her head. "I'm not sure about that. I've caused him nothing but trouble since we met." She tenderly stroked his forehead, pleased to find it warm but not burning.

"I don't think he ever saw it as trouble."

Jenny gave Nelson a pleading look. "He will be all right, won't he Nelson?"

"I've seen the captain in worse battles than this, Mrs. Mortimer. He'll be fine. He has you to come home to."

∞∞∞∞

"Please tell my wife I am going to live and that she is allowed to get some sleep," Richard said as Carmody removed his bandages. Throughout the week of his recovery, Jenny had been a constant presence, nursing him back to health. But it had taken its toll. She looked exhausted.

"Mrs. Mortimer, as your husband's physician, I order you to your bed. You will not be able to do him any good if you fall ill yourself. Do you want to pass some malady onto him in his weakened state?"

"Go, Jenny," Richard said softly. "Go rest."

As soon as Jenny left the room, Mortimer turned to Carmody. "Well?"

"Well, it's healing nicely. I want you to start walking tomorrow. You'll need your man to help you at first, but shortly you'll do with a cane."

"The wound is sore, but I haven't felt the same unrelenting pain that I had before the surgery, so I would say you were successful."

"Oh, I was successful. Your wife will thank me when she realizes just how successful."

"I'm sure my wife is very grateful to you, as am I," Mortimer said.

"Captain, let me be blunt. The ball rested on a nerve, which caused the pain. It also inhibited other natural functions, if I'm not mistaken. You should be able to resume marital relations in a few weeks." Carmody put his instruments back in the black bag he carried.

"Marital relations, I haven't. . ."

"Well, now you will. No need to re-bandage. The air will help it heal. I know Mrs. Mortimer will send for me if I'm needed." With that, Carmody departed and left a stunned Mortimer with the prospect of telling his wife that he may be able to consummate their marriage after all.

He hoped she didn't leave him because of it.

∞∞∞∞

Jenny tried to find a house for them to lease so they could vacate her father's Town house, but she'd waited too long and there was nothing available. She wrote to her father and explained their need to stay. She wasn't sure what she would do if he denied her request. She had visions of him descending on Mayfair with the Watch to throw her and her family into Newgate as trespassers.

Richard got stronger every day and once again walked with the aid of a cane, much as he had when she'd first met him. She had forgotten how tall and imposing he stood when erect, his spine straight as though always at attention.

∞∞∞∞

"It seems Abigail is having her first Season after all," Mortimer said to her one afternoon as he exercised his leg by going up and down the main staircase with Jenny, ever vigilant, following him up the stairs or going down before him so she could catch him should he fall. "You realize that if I lose my balance I will take down the both of us," he said as he began another ascent. "I should hate to crush you in a fall, my dear."

"You just concentrate on what you're doing," Jenny argued. "Let me worry about breaking your fall."

Mortimer took another step up to the second floor. Only twenty more to go. He knew their number by heart, had memorized every crack and crevice on each one. He was determined to be taking them two at a time by month's end.

"Mother tells me we are to attend the Ashfords' ball," he said when he reached the top, panting with exertion. When would this brief exercise not exhaust him? He turned and started down, Jenny leading the way, backwards.

"Letitia and Abigail are attending," Jenny corrected.

"I think we should go also," he said.

"You're not well enough."

"I will be by then. It's nearly a month away. I should be walking without a cane by that time."

"Then you should go to escort Abigail," Jenny conceded.

"And you must come to escort me."

"I've nothing to wear."

"Borrow something of Abigail's. As I understand it, she and my mother have visited every modiste on Bond Street."

"Richard. . ." Mortimer stopped midway down the staircase and looked down at the top of Jenny's head, which she kept bowed so she could watch his feet as he took each step. He tapped his finger on the top of her head to get her to look up at him.

"You will need to go out in Society eventually, Jenny. Go shopping with Mother and Abigail this afternoon and get yourself something suitable to wear. You, my princess, are going to a ball."

Jenny glared at him for a moment and Mortimer thought he had made a tactical error. This woman had defied her father after all. There was every chance she would defy him as well.

"Please, Jenny," he said gently. "Won't you come to the ball with me?"

Jenny couldn't resist him when he asked her in that soft, gentle tone. Especially when she knew he was right. She would have to face Society eventually. It may as well be now. If they cut her, so be it. She would return to Fairleigh with her head held high, knowing she had not been cowed by Society's censure.

With Richard by her side, she could face anything.

∞∞∞∞∞

The Carlisles arrived precisely on the first of May. To Jenny's relief, no constable or watchman accompanied them. Jenny had made sure her parents' and Delia's rooms were readied for them before they arrived. Seeing Delia for the first time in almost a year was wonderful. Jenny hadn't realized how much she missed her sister. Every letter she'd sent Delia had been returned unopened. Delia knew nothing about the baby, had not met her husband.

Seeing her mother gave her the sense of coming home. Even though she'd been living in the house she'd called home before, it hadn't felt like she was home until her mother came in and hugged her. Jenny broke down in tears.

"I love you, Jenny," her mother crooned. "I told your father you had good reason for not wanting to marry Mr. Dawson, but he wouldn't listen. You know how stubborn he is. Now, let me meet your Captain."

Jenny proudly introduced Richard to her parents and sister.

Delia and Abigail immediately became fast friends and retreated to Delia's room to compare wardrobes.

The combined family dined together that evening. Her father was courteous but distant. She knew he was still angry with her for defying him. While grateful to him for letting the Mortimer family use the Town house, she was happy she didn't have to answer to him anymore.

She couldn't imagine Richard ever trying to force her to do something she didn't want to do. He treated her with a respect her father never had. Richard actually listened to her and sought out her opinions. Comparing the two men, she found herself very pleased in her husband.

∞∞∞∞

After dinner, the ladies retired to the drawing room for tea and the gentlemen, Douglas, Richard, and Nelson remained at table to enjoy their port.

"I owe you a debt, Mr. Carlisle, for allowing us the use of your home. I would not have made such a rapid recovery without it."

"I suppose I should be grateful to you, too, Mortimer, for taking Jenny in when she ran away from home. Your man here told me in no uncertain terms when he came to see me in Bath that I was no longer to interfere in her life."

"All the more noble of you to accede to her request for us to use the Town house. I realize I have no right to ask anything more of you, sir, but I would ask one thing. That you support Jenny when she reenters Society as my wife. With your support, no one will dare reject her."

"I have always and continue to want only what is best for Jenny. Unfortunately, she has become a headstrong girl who doesn't agree with me. She would not be having this difficulty with Society if she had done her duty and married Dawson last year. I don't like the man, mind you, and wished better for Jenny, but he was willing to do the honorable thing."

"There is nothing honorable about what Dawson did to Jenny, Mr. Carlisle, and you know it."

"We don't know exactly what happened between them."

"I do." Mortimer did not argue the point. "Jenny told you, too, I believe."

"She told me her version of events, but a man and woman often see things differently. Dawson took her walking out with him as tacit consent. He only did what comes naturally to a man. Jenny ought not to have gone off alone with a man if she wasn't willing to take the consequences."

Mortimer fumed. Fortunately for Douglas Carlisle, he was still recovering from the surgery to his leg or the man would be lying on the ground by now, flattened by a well-placed punch to his jaw. How dear, sweet, kind Jenny had come from this man, he didn't know.

But then, he was glad people didn't judge him by his

own parents.

Nelson cleared his throat uncomfortably, and Mortimer apologized to his friend for speaking of such personal matters in his company.

"I just want to say, sir, that Mrs. Mortimer is a fine woman who would never knowingly tell an untruth. I'd be inclined to believe her."

"I'm not saying Jenny lied," Mr. Carlisle persisted. "Merely that it is a matter of perception."

"So you would perceive that Gerald Dawson had every reason to throw Jenny on the ground and forcibly rape her because she asked to speak to him privately at a ball?" Mortimer should not have been surprised by Carlisle's attitude. He'd seen it enough in the army when men took what they wanted from the local women then tried to justify their actions by insisting the women had thrown themselves at them. Battering themselves in the process, it seemed.

"Jenny came up with that story after Dawson confessed their indiscretion to me and asked for her hand. He was good enough for her to lie with but apparently not good enough for her to marry. She'd set her sights on another and wanted nothing more to do with Gerald Dawson. You can see how I had to force her to do the right thing."

"What I see is a father taking the word of a stranger over that of his own daughter. A man who would do anything to avoid a scandal, even if it meant giving his daughter to the very man who had brutalized her. I am glad that Jenny had the good sense to run away before the two of you had the chance to crush her."

"Now see here, I won't have you talking to me that way in my own house. As her husband, it is appropriate for you to take her side, but as her father, I need to look out for the interests of my entire family. Jenny admitted to leading Gerald Dawson out on the terrace that night, admitted asking him for a moment of privacy. What was the man to think? Certainly not that she wanted to tell him she was no longer interested in him. And if that is what she told him, it is certainly understandable that he would try to change her mind, by whatever means he had available. The man was in love with her and wanted to marry her. It wasn't as though he seduced her then left her. There would be no scandal if Jenny hadn't run away."

Mortimer couldn't listen to any more. "I find that I am weary, sir. Nelson, would you please assist me to my room?"

Nelson took the opportunity Mortimer gave him, though they both knew he no longer needed any assistance getting up the stairs.

"Can you believe the pigheadedness of the man?" Mortimer railed when he and Nelson secluded themselves in his room. "No matter what anyone says, no matter how many times you tell him the truth, he won't see it."

"He has to believe what he wants to believe or else he'll have to admit that he failed to adequately protect his daughter."

"May the Lord save us from pigheaded fathers." Mortimer paced his bedroom, pounding the cane on the floor with each step. "If her own father believes the worst about her, what will the rest of Society think? Poor Jenny, she's being painted as a harlot, as a woman of loose morals and low character." Mortimer stopped pacing and looked at Nelson. "I don't care what Carmody says, I'm taking her back to Fairleigh. I won't subject her to this. I certainly won't force her to go to that blasted ball."

Nelson nodded thoughtfully. "You could do that, I suppose, but then this scandal is going to hang over her head the rest of her life. Do you want her to have to hide away at Fairleigh forever? People can think what they want, but you and Mrs. Mortimer know the truth. In the end, the truth is all that matters."

∞∞∞∞

While the men were discussing Jenny's past scandal over their port, the ladies sipped tea in the drawing room. Delia and Abigail played cards while Letitia worked on her needlepoint. Jenny and her mother sat in a quiet corner and talked.

"I'm so sorry about the baby," Elizabeth said. "Julia wrote me about it."

"I wrote you too," Jenny told her mother.

"I know, dear, but your father was too angry to allow us to correspond."

"Why did he let us use this house, then? Why did he reply to that letter?"

"Why, it was the first letter you wrote to him. You'd written to me and to Delia, but never to your father. And see, when you did, he granted your request. I think he regrets this breach between you two. You were always his favorite, Jenny. He only wanted what was best for you."

"Was it best for me to marry Gerald Dawson after what he'd done to me?"

"Why didn't you come to me and tell me what happened that night? If you had, your father would not have been put in the position of having to accept the man's offer. But since you hadn't told us a thing, Douglas had no choice but to rely on Mr. Dawson's story."

"I was too embarrassed and ashamed to tell you. I needed time to get over the shock of it. Mother, you believe me, don't you? I really didn't encourage Mr. Dawson, I intended to discourage him."

"But you made a serious mistake, Jenny. You went off

alone with a man to whom you were not betrothed. There are serious consequences to such actions. Ladies do not behave in that way."

"I know all about the consequences of my actions, Mother," Jenny said bitterly. "Gentlemen have a code of behavior, too, and Gerald Dawson dishonored that code. He did not behave like a gentleman."

"He did offer to marry you, Jenny. But, it doesn't matter now. You have a fine husband. Captain Mortimer seems to be an upstanding young man. Soon, everyone will forget about you jilting Gerald Dawson and leaving him standing at the altar. Letitia said you've been invited to the Ashfords' ball."

Jenny wanted to share her mother's optimism that the invitation to the Ashfords' ball, addressed to Mr. and Mrs. Richard Mortimer, meant that she was no longer being ostracized by their set. She hoped that when she attended the ball on Richard's arm, no one would mention the fact that less than a year earlier she'd been betrothed to another and ran out on the hastily planned wedding.

She hoped that after these many months, Gerald Dawson's vicious gossip about her was long forgotten.

∞∞∞∞

The morning of the Ashfords' ball, Jenny presented Mortimer with a gift. Out of the long, narrow box delivered from a haberdasher on Bond Street, Mortimer pulled a black lacquered walking stick with a gold-plated tip and a lion's head on the top.

"I thought it would go better with your evening clothes than the sturdy brown cane you use around the house."

"You also knew it would be much less offensive to my dignity. Thank you, Mrs. Mortimer." Richard pulled Jenny to him and kissed her gently on the lips. To her credit, she did not shy away, but she did not respond as he had hoped either.

Carmody's prediction had been accurate. Mortimer had awoken that morning with a very painful erection. He'd wanted to shout for joy but instead hastily got out of bed and went to his changing room to deal with the condition before Jenny noticed.

He was a whole man now and wanted to take his wife to bed in celebration. However, convincing Jenny that marital relations could be enjoyable was going to be a delicate task.

Like any good officer, Mortimer planned his wooing campaign with great care. He would start with an occasional caress, gentle, closed-mouthed kisses, and frequent embraces. Already they spent every night in the same bed and often awoke in the morning entwined. Jenny pulled away as soon as awareness reached her, but many a morning Mortimer enjoyed a few moments of holding her sleeping body close. Those moments were heaven to him.

"I have a gift for you, too," he said, going to the dresser and retrieving a small box from the top drawer. "I never gave you a betrothal ring. I hope you like this."

Jenny opened the box to reveal a beautiful sapphire ring surrounded by diamonds. "It's beautiful. Oh, Richard, thank you. You didn't need to give this to me. You've done so much for me already." For the first time in their married life, Jenny initiated an embrace and even went up on tiptoe to plant a light kiss on his cheek.

"Not nearly as much as I intend to give you, Jenny." He kissed her forehead and had to stop himself from proceeding further and kissing his way down her face to her neck and the tops of her breasts, which peeked invitingly from the top of her bodice. God, he wanted his wife. He felt like a randy schoolboy discovering erotic passions for the first time. Like an untried schoolboy, he had no control over his body. He moved away from Jenny before she could detect his erection and take it as a betrayal.

"I trust you've found something suitable to wear this evening?" Mortimer was still unsure about the wisdom of taking Jenny to the Ashfords' ball, even though he had insisted they accept the invitation. But as the day of the ball had drawn near, he watched Jenny's excitement grow.

He remembered her telling him how much she had been enjoying her first Season before her betrothal to Gerald Dawson cut it short. She deserved the opportunity to dance again.

"Fortunately, Lady Taunton is increasing and could no longer fit into the gown she'd ordered several months ago. She and I are the same size and have similar coloring, so the seamstress was only too happy to tailor it for me and give it to me for half the price."

"I am not a poor man, Jenny. I assure you I could have paid the full cost."

Jenny laughed, a lilting, sunny sound that he had heard far too seldom in their short acquaintance. "I'm afraid I am my father's daughter in some respects and this is one of them. I am a bit of a penny pincher."

"If that is your worst trait, wife of mine, I consider myself the most fortunate of men."

Jenny looked at him as though seeing him for the first time. Their short marriage had been characterized by one crisis after another, but here they were now bantering like an old married couple. A couple who had married for love, not convenience.

"I hope you are pleased in your choice of wife," she said, then added demurely, "as I am by my choice of husband."

"I am well pleased, Jenny," he assured her. Jenny smiled and for the first time it seemed that the heavy load of sorrow she had carried since their first meeting dissipated. This was the Jenny that Dawson had seen and wanted. And destroyed.

In that instant, Mortimer knew he could not hurt her and would not betray her. Even if it meant living as a celibate the rest of his life. If Jenny could not come willingly to his bed, he would never force her, not even through gentle coercion. Consummating their marriage would have to be her idea, her initiative.

Which made bedding his wife an even bigger challenge than he had at first anticipated..

TEN

The Ashfords were good ton but not high ton. Their guest list consisted largely of an assortment of low gentry, a few baronets, men of law and of medicine, commissioned officers and former officers, and men of business who were discreet enough to mingle with the aristocracy. The coup of the evening for Cornelia Ashford was getting Lady Carmilla Dunston to attend. Lady Dunston was the widow of Lord Dunston, late of India, and a woman of influence who had graced the ballrooms of Dukes and Earls. Having her attend a function put on by a mere Mrs. was indeed a social victory. Since Mrs. Ashford had made it commonly known Lady Dunston would attend, her ball was the crush of the evening. Even those who had previously made other plans changed them so they could mingle with nobility.

Not the occasion Jenny would have chosen to make her first appearance in Society since leaving it so ignominiously the previous Season. Everyone who was anyone in her world would be in attendance. The gentlemen she had flirted with and who had courted her last year would be there. The girls she had gossiped with and competed for male attention with would also be there. As would their mothers who were ever ready to judge and pronounce their judgments loudly and repeatedly to anyone within hearing.

As she waited for their carriage to take its turn at the curb to disgorge its passengers, Jenny's hands sweated inside her over-the-elbow kid gloves.

She was scared. She shook with an unreasoning fear, having nothing to do with who would be there and what they might say. The mere act of attending a ball frightened her. Any ball, not just this one.

Her last ball had ended in disaster. Her last ball had been the scene of such ugliness she never allowed her mind to review it. As the carriage pulled up in front of the Ashfords' front door, Jenny started shaking uncontrollably. She couldn't catch her breath and took gasping gulps of air that refused to fill her lungs.

Richard, seated across from her, took note of her anxiety. He reached a hand out to her just as a footman flung the carriage door open. He jumped down and reached up to lift her out of the carriage, but she remained frozen in her seat.

"Go on, girl," Letitia, seated next to her, nudged her toward the door. Abigail, who had been seated next to Richard in the rear-facing seat, took the initiative and accepted his waiting hand. Letitia practically shoved Jenny out the door.

Richard steadied her when she reached the ground and kept her beside him while he assisted his mother in disembarking. Offering Jenny his elbow, he directed Letitia and Abigail with his walking stick to precede them up the front steps.

"Hold on tight, Jenny," he whispered. "I won't leave you."

Fortified by Richard's strength, Jenny lifted her chin and prepared to face whatever awaited her—welcome, censure, or bad memories.

To her utter surprise and relief, everyone she met greeted her. Mrs. Ashford was indeed Letitia Mortimer's dear friend and as such welcomed Letitia's family as honored guests. She was Jenny Carlisle no longer, but Mrs. Richard Mortimer and as such received utmost respect as the wife of a revered military hero.

It was as though the events of last Season had never taken place.

For the duration of this evening, Jenny determined to do her best to pretend they hadn't. She wiped from her mind all thoughts of that last ball and instead remembered the first ball she ever attended. She had only to see the wonder in Abigail's eyes to relive that earlier experience when she, too, had been fresh and young. And naïve.

Delia grabbed Abigail as soon as she spotted her and the two girls went off to join a bevy of pastel-bedecked beauties hovering on the edge of the dance floor. Looking at their youthful innocence, Jenny found it hard to fathom that just last year she had been one of them. She felt old, jaded, and downright matronly. Yet, oddly happy.

Richard was not yet able to dance, so Jenny had resolved to spend the evening standing at his side. Richard, however, had other plans. She wasn't quite sure how he engineered it, but before the music even started, every dance had been claimed by some gentleman of Richard's acquaintance, with Richard's permission of course.

As she took her place for the first set, escorted by Major Anthony Gray, Richard's former superior officer, Jenny was transported back, not to the anguish of her last ball, but to the joys of all the ones that preceded it. She remembered how much she loved to dance, especially with an experienced partner, as Major Gray proved to be.

Even better than in her first Season was the fact that she did not have to flirt or try to engage the Major's interest in her. What little conversation they had centered on topics of mutual interest—the quality of the musicians, the lovely decorations, and most importantly, Richard's recuperation. She could relax and enjoy herself without having to worry about the awkward silence or encouraging a potential suitor.

Because she was not a husband-hunting Miss this Season but a very married Mrs.

Wherever the steps of the dance took her, her eyes always found Richard. He was by far the most handsome man in the room with his broad shoulders, chestnut hair and trim mustache that gave him a dashing, dangerous appearance. His blue eyes followed her as her steps traced the intricate pattern of the dance. Whenever she looked up and caught his eye, he was ready with a smile for her. It filled her with a warm, secure feeling knowing that Richard watched her.

The first set ended and Major Gray returned her to Richard's side. They shared a quiet moment before her next partner claimed her.

"Are you enjoying yourself?" Richard inquired.

"Very much so. Thank you for coercing all your friends to partner me."

"Believe me, no coercion was necessary. You look beautiful tonight, absolutely radiant." The compliment, coupled with the heated way Richard looked at her, made her blush. Jenny waved her fan in an attempt to cool down her flushed face. She felt nervous and giddy all of a sudden, almost the way she'd felt last summer when a gentleman paid her particular attention.

And then it dawned on her. Her husband was flirting

with her.

She was saved from having to respond when the orchestra struck up the chords to the next dance and her partner claimed her.

He devoured her with his eyes. In fact, Richard's unrelenting gaze so distracted her, Jenny missed a step and almost tripped over Mr. Alan Gordon's feet. It was the last dance before the midnight supper break, and she had danced each and every one save the waltz, from which she cried off on the premise that her feet needed the rest. In truth, she didn't want any man save Richard to hold her that intimately close.

Now he watched her with a look that was more than merely possessive, it was nearly primitive. Throughout the evening, each time she returned to his side, Richard had made her heart flutter and her stomach feel like she had swallowed butterflies. By a heated look, sweet word, or accidental caress, he had her blushing and giggling like the gaggle of girls Abigail and Delia were with. Jenny felt foolish and a bit silly, yet she reveled in Richard's attentions.

Now this. The way he looked at her across the crowded dance floor could only be described as ravenous. Her stomach did a little flip-flop and she nearly lost her footing again.

If she didn't know better, she would suspect that Richard desired her.

But Richard was incapable of desire, for which she was grateful. Wasn't she? Of course she was.

She'd loved Richard for months, but it was the kind of love she felt for a friend and protector. He was her hero. Larger than life. She'd never really seen him as a man.

Until tonight. Until he caressed her with his eyes and made promises with his smile. Promises he was not able to keep. Promises she didn't want him to keep.

She didn't want to feel the tickle of his mustache as he kissed her the way he had that morning. She didn't need the solid weight of his arm across her belly at night when he was sound asleep, a comforting yet strangely exciting closeness she was always careful to distance herself from at the first blush of dawn.

Jenny was safe with Richard. There was no danger of him wanting things—demanding things—that she was unable to give. That she would never be able to give, even if her heart did race when he looked at her like that.

∞∞∞∞

Watching Jenny dance with other men made Mortimer crazy. Even though it was his idea, even though he had personally approved every man she partnered with, he couldn't stand the thought of anyone but him holding her close. At least she had refused to dance the waltz. He hadn't insisted.

The next ball they attended he would be partnering her himself. To hell with what people said, he intended to dance every last dance with his wife. His beautiful, desirable wife.

He couldn't help following her with his eyes. As far as he was concerned, she was the only woman in the room. She danced gracefully, slim and sleek with a natural ability to flow with the music. Except for the occasional misstep when she caught him looking at her.

Wanting her.

Mortimer tried to school his expression. It would not do for every man in the room to know how much he desired his wife.

It would not do for her to realize that his desire was very real and very physical.

Alan Gordon returned her to him after the last dance.

Gordon was an old friend who had bought his commission at the same time as Mortimer. Gordon had had the good sense to cash in his commission after only two years. Military life had not agreed with him—he'd come home and married an heiress who was at home awaiting the birth of their fourth child.

"You have a lovely wife, Mortimer," Gordon said as he placed Jenny's hand into Mortimer's. "Pretty soon you'll have a brood like mine."

Gordon bowed and went off to find a suitable young lady to escort into supper.

"Your friend Mr. Gordon is a delightful dancer, but I'm afraid he spends far too much time around his children," Jenny commented. "He kept talking to me as though I were two."

Mortimer laughed. It was so good to see Jenny happy. How she ever thought that her younger sister Delia outshone her, he didn't know. To him, Delia was naught but a pale imitation of Jenny, lacking her strength, her color, her liveliness.

Jenny may not have been the Incomparable of last year's Season, but she certainly must have had a large number of suitors. He hoped she would not regret tying herself to him once she realized she could have had her choice of husband.

As he'd stood on the side watching the dancers, he'd kept his ear tuned to the slightest unkind word about her. He'd heard none. It would seem that Jenny's fears were unfounded. No one censured her for running away from Gerald Dawson. In fact, there were a few who thought she'd made the best decision.

Of course, he made it very clear that theirs was a love match. If he implied that Jenny had left Dawson for him, because she knew he was returning home a wounded hero who needed her attention, so be it. No one needed to know that they met at an inn on the road to Bath on a rain soaked night.

Mortimer escorted Jenny to the table where Letitia and Abigail were seated. An awkward young man with overlarge teeth sat on Abigail's right. He looked no older than ten, but Abigail appeared quite enamored of him. The young man jumped up when they arrived and held out his hand to Mortimer.

"Clive Hallworth, Captain. It's a pleasure to meet you. May I get you and your lady something from the buffet table?"

Mortimer hated to quash the overeager puppy so allowed him to fetch and carry for them. In truth, his leg hurt from standing for so long, and he was grateful to avoid the line at the supper table.

As soon as young Mr. Hallworth departed, Carmody took his place.

"Why Mr. Carmody, I wasn't aware you were here this evening," Jenny said.

"Just arrived, Mrs. Mortimer. I wanted to check on my prize patient." His gaze, however, rested on Abigail rather than Richard.

"I haven't danced yet, but the walking is getting better every day."

"Good, good," Carmody replied, clearly distracted by Abigail's teeth biting into a chicken croquette. "Have you danced this evening, Miss Mortimer?"

"I've enjoyed several dances, though Mother would not allow me to dance the waltz. She said I was too young for such a scandalous exhibition. Do you dance?"

Jenny coughed at Abigail's blatant angling for an invitation.

"I'm afraid I have two left feet when it comes to dancing, Miss Mortimer. However, I do a very fine turn about the dining room. Would you care to join me?" He

extended his arm and Abigail accepted without hesitation.

"Carmody and Abigail?" Jenny laughed. "I never would have thought it."

Richard was not pleased.

"He's too old for her," he complained when they'd left the table to take their stroll about the room.

"He's younger than you, dear," Letitia put in. She appeared to approve of the surgeon's attentions.

"Must be the beard that ages him, then."

"I much prefer a man with a mustache," Jenny said.

Poor Clive Hallworth returned to discover that the object of his affection had abandoned him for another man. He plopped their plates on the table and went off to join a group of young men heading for the smoking room.

Jenny absently watched him walk away, which was the only reason her gaze turned toward the smoking room at that moment. The man exiting it into the dining room looked her directly in the eye. Jenny blanched. Gerald Dawson. She dropped the fork she had picked up in preparation of attacking the dinner plate Hallworth had brought for her. It clanged noisily.

Mortimer looked at Jenny in alarm. She'd gone pale and looked as if she were likely to faint. Following her gaze, his eyes settled on Dawson, who had the audacity to head right for them.

Mortimer stood, blocking Dawson from reaching Jenny.

"Good evening, Captain," Dawson said when he reached their table. "I believe felicitations are in order. Congratulations on your marriage." He bowed politely. Mortimer did not return the courtesy but stared at Dawson in stony silence.

Undeterred, Dawson leaned around Mortimer so he could see Jenny where she remained seated behind him.

"I'm glad to find you well, Mrs. Mortimer," he said. Holding his hand out to Mortimer, Dawson added, "No hard feelings, my good man."

Mortimer looked at the proffered hand as though it were a vile putrefaction. He did not take it.

Dawson shrugged and retracted it, seemingly unconcerned with the insult until he declared in a voice loud enough for all those in the vicinity to hear, "Don't blame me, old man. I could have told you she was a disappointment in the bedroom, but I didn't think it was necessary since you tried her yourself at the Cock and Hen on the Bath road. Though I admit, I too was willing to marry her. Her father's money is an enticement."

If Dawson expected Mortimer to hit him and cause a scene, he was surely disappointed. With his officer's calm, Mortimer stared Dawson down as he had many an insubordinate.

"I believe, sir, that you just insulted not only me, but my wife. What say you, sir?"

"Oh, I meant no insult, Captain. I was simply commiserating on our shared taste in women." Dawson leaned in and added confidentially, "She's a bit of a screamer, isn't she."

Mortimer smiled and turned to Jenny, hoping she hadn't heard Dawson's last comment.

"Will you excuse us, my dear? Mr. Dawson and I have something we need to discuss.".

ELEVEN

"Well, Dawson, what's your pleasure? Pistols or bare knuckles? You did intend to goad me into calling you out, didn't you?" They stood in a quiet corner of the smoking room though they were without doubt the center of attention. Conversations stopped all around them, and ears perked to catch their interchange.

"Dueling is illegal, Captain, or have you forgotten? However, were I to meet you on the field of honor, my preference would be rapiers."

Mortimer nodded.

"And exactly which field would you select for such a meeting, were dueling not illegal, that is?"

"Why, everyone knows that the meadow at Longbridge Crossing is ideally suited for such assignations and was used with astonishing frequency back before dueling was outlawed."

"I believe my man Nelson may know of the place," Mortimer said conversationally. "I shall ask him. Do you have any friends, Dawson?"

"Why, I believe there are one or two good fellows I could call on to stand as my friends." Dawson scanned the gentlemen gathered in the room.

"I'll stand as your friend, Dawson," Cornelius Hayes shouted from across the room.

"And I," said Steward Lane.

"Well, well," came a sardonic voice from the doorway. "It seems you would have all the elements you needed for a duel, were dueling not illegal. All save the services of a surgeon, that is. I, of course, could never lend my services to such an endeavor, believing strongly as I do that dueling is a wasteful indulgence of the aristocracy of whom I do not count myself a part. However, since this is a mere hypothetical discussion, then I can hypothetically propose myself as the surgeon to have on hand for such a hypothetical event." Carmody strolled over to stand beside Mortimer. "How glad I am that you are not planning on fighting a duel in fact, Captain, because I would hate to see you ruin my fine handiwork."

Mortimer shook Carmody's hand. "I trust you returned my sister safely to her mother and sister-in-law."

"As any true gentleman would," Carmody replied with a telling glance at Dawson. It seemed, Mortimer realized, that Dawson's mistreatment of Jenny was not the secret she had thought it. Dawson may have spread his own version of the truth, but most people were discerning enough to recognize it for the falsehood it was. Anyone who knew Jenny, at least.

Perhaps with the exception of her own father. Mortimer noted Douglas Carlisle sitting across the room with several men of a similar age. He pretended disinterest in the conversation taking place in the corner, but Mortimer knew he'd heard every word and understood Mortimer was doing what he should have done the previous year—seeking justice for Jenny.

"It is too bad that dueling is illegal," Dawson said in a low, mean tone. "For I would like nothing better than to meet you on the field of honor tomorrow at dawn for stealing away my fiancée."

"Your fiancée didn't require stealing," Mortimer rejoined. "She ran away quite well on her own."

"It being after midnight already and technically already the morning of a new day," Carmody said. "Do you mean by 'tomorrow' this very morning, or what would actually be tomorrow morning?" Dawson looked at Carmody in confusion.

"This ball began on Friday night," Mortimer clarified. "Would you wish to meet at dawn on Saturday or Sunday? One must be very specific about these things. It would not do to be called coward simply because one got one's dates mixed up."

"Saturday," Dawson stammered. Then, regaining is bravado, sneered. "I would not want to wait another day before seeing you dead."

"One of us would be dead, but it would not necessarily be me," Mortimer pointed out.

Dawson looked pointedly at the walking stick Mortimer leaned on. "I ensured victory by choosing rapiers," he said smugly.

"So you think." Mortimer smiled and Dawson lost some of his confidence.

∞∞∞∞

By the time the gentlemen returned to the ballroom, the room was abuzz with talk of the duel. Though everyone was careful to say that no actual duel would take place, the exact details of the plan were passed from person to person.

Jenny knew better than anyone that the duel was real. She feared for Richard, but she couldn't help feeling satisfied. Finally, someone had the courage to stand up for her against Gerald Dawson. If her father had done so last year, she could have saved Richard from having to fight her battle for her. Not that she thought her father should have called Gerald Dawson out. But he needn't have given in to the man's demands.

If her father had believed her and taken her side, Gerald Dawson would have been ostracized at the very least. At most, he could have been brought before the courts.

But her father had chosen appeasement. Her father had chosen to blame her for Dawson's heinous behavior. Her father had chosen to believe the worst about her rather than defend her.

Her husband made no such choice. Jenny's heart filled with pride for him. And such love. Here was a man who would defend his family at whatever cost. Richard would never allow a daughter of his to suffer the indignities that Jenny had suffered. How sad that he would never have the opportunity to be a father because she knew he would be a good one.

However, as gratified as she was by Richard's willingness to defend her, she could not allow him to do so. His leg was still healing and there was too much risk. She would not lose him to someone like Gerald Dawson. Her honor was not worth the cost.

∞∞∞∞

They could not talk about it on the drive home because Delia and Abigail rode in their carriage with them. Letitia had joined the Carlisles in theirs.

"How did you enjoy your first ball?" Mortimer asked Abigail once the girls stopped giggling long enough for him to voice his question.

"It was wonderful. Better than I'd even dreamed.

Thank you, Richard, and you Jenny, for making this night possible. Mr. Carmody promised to come call tomorrow," she added shyly.

"Carmody is a good man," Mortimer assured her. "However, wouldn't you be happier being courted by someone closer to your own age. Clive Hallworth seemed like a nice young man."

"Clive Hallworth has big teeth," Abigail complained. "Besides, Mr. Carmody is no older than I than you are older than Jenny."

"That's different," Mortimer limply explained.

"How is it different? You are eight years older than Jenny and Mr. Carmody is eight years older than I."

"I didn't seek Jenny out to marry her, I married her because I had to, because she needed me too," Mortimer said, clearly flustered. "I certainly would not have courted a woman her age by choice, and certainly not a girl your age."

The other inhabitants of the carriage sat in stunned silence.

"You didn't want to marry Jenny?" Delia asked, ready to defend her sister against such an aspersion.

"What do you mean you had to marry her?" Abigail picked up on that tidbit. "Are the rumors we heard all night true? Were you—improper—before your marriage?"

Jenny hadn't said a word and Mortimer was afraid to look at her for fear he had hurt her. He felt her shaking next to him she was so upset, and he wished they were alone so he could explain that he'd misspoken.

Of course he'd wanted to marry her. Had wanted to marry her then and wanted to remain married to her now. She had to know that. Didn't she?

Then why was she crying? He glanced over at her. Her hands covered her face, but she wasn't crying. She was laughing. Jenny was laughing at him.

Mortimer started laughing, too. "You could have tried to save me," he said.

"You were doing far too good a job digging that hole for yourself." Jenny laughed. Then she turned to Delia and Abigail.

"What the captain meant was that neither of us was looking for marriage when we met, but circumstance forced us to see each other in a different light. I think it is the best kind of marriage that begins from a mutual respect and admiration."

"That's exactly what I meant." Mortimer gripped the lifeline she'd thrown him and climbed. "And Jenny and I did nothing improper before our wedding," he told Abigail emphatically.

We did nothing improper before the wedding nor after, he added silently to himself. There was significant irony to that. Something he would do his best to change in the near future.

Should he survive the duel he was not fighting with Dawson in the morning.

"You're not meeting him," Jenny said as soon as their bedroom door closed behind them. "I won't let you."

Mortimer would have liked to have seen her try to stop him, but she'd probably use some womanly trick like crying and would succeed. So he did what every self-respecting gentleman would do in such a situation—he lied.

"The talk of a duel was just that—talk. Though I would like nothing better than to meet that odious man in physical combat and return him to Hades from whence he no doubt spawned, he is too much the coward to ever consent to such a meeting. You have nothing to fear on my account, my love."

"Still, I shall sleep by your side as usual tonight and

will know should you leave me."

Mortimer pulled Jenny into his arms and lightly kissed her cheek.

"I will never leave you, Jenny."

∞∞∞∞

Mortimer crept downstairs in his robe and bare feet. Nelson met him in the kitchen and provided him with suitable clothing for a meeting at dawn. With any luck, they'd be well on their way to Longbridge Crossing before Jenny awoke and realized that he had gone.

"His seconds paid me a visit last night," Nelson confided. "Bloody coward thinks he can best you in a sword fight does he? Isn't he in for a surprise."

"He may be right, Nelson," Mortimer said as he pulled on his boot. "I haven't fenced since I took the musket ball in this leg."

Nelson just looked at him as though he were a bloody fool.

"It isn't fencing we call it on the battlefield, Captain. It's survival. I've seen you take down seasoned men with your sword. One scurrilous jackanapes isn't going to best you, sir."

Mortimer looked up to the ceiling, thinking of Jenny upstairs in their bed. "I hope you're right Nelson. I hope you're right."

∞∞∞∞

Jenny waited until she was sure Richard and Nelson were gone before she got up and got dressed. Before leaving the house, she went to her father's desk in the study. In the bottom drawer, she found the pistol he kept for household protection. Taking shot and powder, she concealed the pistol in the deep pocket of her cloak. She would load it when she reached Longbridge Crossing and use it if she had to.

Like the morning she had run away from her impending marriage to Gerald Dawson, Jenny let herself out the back door and walked the ten blocks to Whitechurch Street where she could hire a Hansom cab. The sky was already lightening and she feared she might be too late.

If he hurt Richard, Gerald Dawson would answer to her.

∞∞∞∞

Carmody was there when Mortimer and Nelson arrived, but they had to wait for Dawson and his seconds to appear.

"Any chance he might have run off to the continent and saved us all the trouble?" Carmody asked when fifteen minutes had elapsed with still no sign of Dawson.

"I doubt it. He wanted this duel for some reason. Maybe he thinks that with me out of the way, he can still marry Jenny."

"Over my dead body," Nelson said.

"Actually, Nelson, that would be over mine. But, even if Jenny is widowed, there is no chance she will ever marry Gerald Dawson. And if she is widowed, she won't need to marry anyone if she doesn't want to. I've made sure she will be well taken care of for the rest of her life. I trust you will see to her protection."

"That won't be necessary, Captain. You'll be here to do that yourself."

"Here they come." Carmody spotted the approaching carriage.

"Good morning, gentlemen," Cornelius Hayes greeted them cheerfully as he descended from the carriage. He staggered slightly and caught himself from falling face first on the cold, hard ground by grabbing the carriage door.

"Looks as if they stayed up all night drinking," Nelson said incredulously.

"This isn't going to be a duel," Carmody commented. "It will be a massacre."

Dawson approached with a swaggering step. He bowed to the three assembled.

"Gentlemen." Dawson didn't appear to be as drunk as his seconds, Mortimer was relieved to see. He knew that drink slowed a man's reaction time, but it also made men dangerous. He had no doubt Dawson would be a mean drunk who would think nothing of incorporating underhanded tactics.

He had some underhanded tactics of his own to call on as well if needed.

Steward Lane staggered over under the weight of a sword case. He placed it gently on the ground and opened it to reveal two weapons.

"Would you care to select your weapon?" Dawson asked Mortimer.

"No thank you, I brought my own." Mortimer wore his scabbard and his battle trusted sword. No gentleman's sporting piece like the pretty rapiers Dawson had provided but a soldier's weapon that felt familiar and set well in his hand. He wouldn't trust any sword Dawson gave him, it was likely to have a filed down tip that would not penetrate a man's skin.

Mortimer removed his scabbard and withdrew his sword. It had drawn blood before and likely would again this morning. Nelson had sharpened it and made it shine. Mortimer tried a flourish and it felt like an old friend in his hand.

Dawson selected a sword from the case, tried it and

found it lacking. He replaced it and drew out the second. It seemed to satisfy him because he stepped back and said, "En garde."

Mortimer had never been a gifted fencer. He did not have refined moves and did not spar effortlessly. He was a soldier. To him, fencing was not a sport, it was combat. He fought as he always did, without finesse but with practiced skill. Mortimer did not waste time or effort on parries and fakes. He went in for the kill.

Dawson made the first move, a lightning quick jab that a fencing master would likely meet with a block and parry. Mortimer didn't do the expected. Instead, before Dawson had a chance to shift his weight to his back leg to receive the anticipated blow, Mortimer stepped in with a jab of his own. Dawson lost his balance and fell backwards, landing hard on the ground with the wind knocked right out of him. Before he could recover his wits, Mortimer planted his foot on Dawson's sword hand and touched his sword point to Dawson's throat.

The fight was over in less than a minute.

"I won't kill you, though it would delight me to do so," Mortimer said, pushing the sharp point so that it nicked Dawson's skin, drawing blood. "I do demand an apology for my wife, though what you did to her no apology can ever remedy."

"I apologize," Dawson croaked, trying to push his head into the ground to put some distance between his vulnerable, exposed throat and Mortimer's sword point.

"What, specifically, are you apologizing for?" Mortimer said in a soft, deadly voice.

"Whatever offense I may have caused," Dawson tried.

"Specifically," Mortimer reiterated.

"I forced her. I am sorry I forced her. She did not come with me willingly. She was rejecting me. I couldn't let her. I had to marry her. Her father's rich as Croesus and I've lost everything." Tears leaked from the corners of Dawson's eyes and wetness spread on the front of his breeches. He was looking death in the eye and he knew it.

Mortimer hesitated, sorely tempted to thrust the sword point home and end Dawson's miserable life.

"That will do." Mortimer pulled up the sword and all those assembled let out their breaths. Hayes and Lane came over to help their comrade stand. "One more thing. Nelson, will you please escort Mr. Dawson down to the docks and see that he is impressed into service on one of His Majesty's ships? I believe that will solve all of your difficulties, Mr. Dawson. You will earn a respectable pay and you will be somewhere that I won't be able to kill you."

"You can't do that!" Dawson objected. "I'm a gentleman. You can't have me thrown in with the rabble."

"The rabble you should be thrown in with is the rabble at Newgate," Mortimer said sternly. "You deserve to be hung for rape, Dawson. What I am giving you is better than you deserve."

∞∞∞∞

Jenny watched from her hiding place behind a nearby tree. She'd left the hired cab down the road apiece and had walked unseen close to the group in the meadow. She had just reached the tree when the fight began. Had she blinked, she would have missed it as it was over in an instant. One moment Dawson thrust a jab at Richard, the next he was on the ground with Richard's sword at his throat.

She loosened the grip on the loaded pistol she held at her side. It would not be needed. Richard had things well in hand.

She couldn't hear what they were saying. For a moment, she feared Richard would allow his emotions to reign and slice Dawson's neck with his sword. But she should have known better. Richard was an officer. He would never act dishonorably. Killing a disarmed man as he lay helplessly on the ground was not something Richard would ever do.

She could not say the same for herself. She leveled the pistol and aimed it at Dawson's head.

TWELVE

Only the fear that she might accidentally hit one of the bystanders stayed her from taking the shot.

She lowered the gun and dropped it on the ground, shocked by the murderous intent she had felt. This was what Gerald Dawson had created, this was what he'd reduced her to. She had never known she was capable of feeling such hatred, such loathing.

But killing Dawson would not bring back her virginity. It would not repair what he had broken. It would only destroy her more. It would be the destruction of her very soul.

Sliding to the ground, Jenny leaned her back against the trunk of the tree and started to shake like she had a chill. She'd almost killed a man. She'd had her finger on the trigger, the pistol was loaded, primed, and ready. If Dawson had been alone, or if he had presented a better target, she would have killed him. Without thought. Without regret. Not to protect Richard as she had told herself all the way here. But to avenge herself.

She wanted to feel power over Gerald Dawson the way he'd held it over her. She wanted him to feel vulnerable and afraid the way he'd made her feel.

But more than that, she wanted him dead. The only way she would ever feel safe again was if Gerald Dawson was dead.

She should have married him after all. Then she could easily have murdered him in his sleep.

The thought made her laugh, a high-pitched, hysterical sound that she couldn't stop.

∞∞∞∞

The departing carriages drowned out the sound of Jenny's laughter as first Hayes and Lane left the scene, then Nelson and a reluctant Dawson exited in Mortimer's carriage. Mortimer himself had accepted Carmody's offer to drive him back to the Carlisle Town house. The possibility of catching Abigail at breakfast might have influenced Carmody's generosity.

Mortimer was about to step into the carriage when he heard an unusual birdcall from behind a nearby tree. No, it wasn't a bird. It was a person. Laughing. Though the laughter had more madness in it than joy.

He recognized it right away. He'd heard that kind of laughter before, on the battlefield after the fighting was over and men were left to witness their own brutality.

"Wait a moment, please," Mortimer said to Carmody. He walked over to the tree, limping painfully in the uneven ground of the meadow, having forgotten to bring either cane or walking stick for his dawn meeting.

A hint of blue fabric peeked out from behind the tree. As he came closer, he saw it was part of a skirt complemented by a matching jacket. He recognized the outfit as Jenny's riding habit an instant before he recognized the laughter as Jenny's. It wasn't her usual laugh, though. This was more of the hysterical variety.

"Jenny," he said sharply. The laughter stopped immediately. Mortimer leaned one hand against the tree trunk and looked down on the top of her head. She didn't move. "Jenny, please stand up and talk to me. I'd kneel down to you, but I fear I would not be able to rise again."

Slowly, Jenny stood, but she kept her back to him. Something caught his attention on the ground. Her skirt had been covering it, but when she stood, it was revealed. A pistol.

Using the tree for balance, Mortimer leaned down and retrieved it. With the skill of an experienced marksman, he quickly unloaded the shot and disarmed it. He tucked the pistol into the waistband of his pants.

"I wanted to kill him." Jenny spoke softly, still facing away from him, so that he could barely catch her words. Mortimer placed a hand on her shoulder and gently turned her around. "I told myself I was coming to protect you, that I would only shoot if he hurt you, but when you had him pinned to the ground and I saw that you weren't going to follow through, that you weren't going to shove the point of your sword into his throat, I raised the pistol and aimed at him. Every fiber of my being wanted to pull the trigger."

"But you didn't."

"Only because I was afraid I'd hurt someone else."

"Are you disappointed in me, that I didn't finish it? Did you want me to kill him?"

"I knew you wouldn't, not that way. You are too honorable to kill a man you have disarmed."

She had never seen him in battle. He remembered a number of times when he'd sent his bayonet home into an enemy not caring whether the man carried a weapon or not. He was not as honorable as Jenny supposed him to be.

"I did not kill him because dueling is illegal, and I

would have been convicted for murder. Believe me, I wanted to pierce him with my sword with every fiber of my being. The man is unfit to live. But I would not put that stain on you or my family."

"You see, you are honorable."

"Jenny, wanting to kill a man and actually doing it are two very different things. I am glad you didn't shoot him. I would not have you bear that burden. I've seen enough killing. Done enough killing. More than enough for both of us."

"What happens the next time he taunts us? The next time I encounter him in a ballroom? When will I ever be free of him?"

"Just because I didn't kill him doesn't mean I will allow him to bother you again. Gerald Dawson is about to begin an illustrious career in His Majesty's Navy. Nelson is seeing to it. You will never lay eyes on the man again, Jenny."

Jenny closed her eyes, in relief he hoped. But when she opened them, she pierced him with a stony, determined gaze. "This is the last time I allow you to fight my battles for me, Richard. From now on, I stand on my own."

He gave her a mock bow. "Very well, madam wife. The next duel is yours to fight."

With that, he turned and limped back toward the waiting carriage.

Jenny watched him go. He was angry with her. He had every right. Here he'd risked his life for her and she, ungrateful wench that she was, criticized him for it, first for not killing Dawson when he had the chance, then for fighting him in the first place. Jenny looked around for the pistol, then realized that Richard had taken it. Just as well, at this moment, she might be tempted to use it on herself. Feeling foolish and not wanting to endure Richard's accusing silence all the way back to London,

Jenny hiked back to the road at the point where she'd left the hired carriage. It was gone, of course. Too much time had passed, the coachman decided she wasn't coming back even though she'd paid him extra to wait.

She had walked from Bath to Fairleigh, she could walk from Longbridge Crossing to London. Perhaps in the time it took, she would think of something to say to Richard when she got home.

A half hour passed before Mortimer accepted that Jenny was not going to follow him to the carriage.

"She must have made her own way back to Town, she got out here on her own after all."

"Mrs. Mortimer is a very resourceful lady," Carmody agreed. "She made sure you were well taken care of after your surgery."

Mortimer nodded and immediately felt guilty for leaving her alone at the tree, but he was so angry at her he had to walk away before he said something he would regret. Didn't she understand that he wanted to fight her battles for her? He loved her, damn it. What else did he have to give if not his protection? Nothing else she would accept. Certainly not the passion he longed to share with her. Passion he feared she would never be ready to enjoy.

Maybe he should have killed Dawson. The man deserved it. He'd ruined not only Jenny's life, but now Mortimer's life as well. Because he wanted to make love to his wife and because of Gerald Dawson, Jenny didn't want to be touched by him or any other man.

They had traveled only a short distance when Mortimer saw a familiar patch of blue on the road up ahead.

"I am going to kill her," he muttered as he signaled the coachman to stop. "Mrs. Mortimer, please join us in this carriage at once," he called down to her when the carriage came to a halt beside her.

"Very well, Captain," Jenny agreed. She wasn't walking to be stubborn after all. She was walking out of necessity. "The coach I hired left before I got back," she explained when she climbed in assisted by Mortimer's outreached hand.

An uncomfortable silence descended upon the occupants.

"I hope we are back in time for breakfast," Carmody said in an attempt to lighten the mood.

Mortimer grunted.

Jenny continued to stare out the window.

"Awfully glad my services weren't needed this morning," Carmody tried again.

Both Mortimers ignored him and Carmody gave up.

"Do come in for breakfast, Mr. Carmody," Jenny said when they reached the Town house. She leaped out as soon as a footman opened the carriage door and disappeared inside.

"By all means, Carmody, make yourself at home." Mortimer followed his wife at a much slower pace. Carmody decided that this morning might not be the best time to pay court to Miss Abigail after all.

"Take me home, John," he ordered his driver.

∞∞∞∞

Mortimer stopped by the dining room, but it was empty. Breakfast hadn't even been laid out yet. He looked at the mantle clock and saw that it was only half seven. His dawn appointment had taken a little more than two hours. The rest of the household hadn't even risen from their beds yet.

He passed a maid on the way up to his room and ordered a bath.

"Mrs. Mortimer has already asked for one," the girl

said.

Jenny waited for him in the room they'd shared since her parents had descended on the house and she'd moved her things out of their room. Since she'd been sleeping in his bed anyway, it was a mere formality. He wondered if she realized how unusual it was for married couples of their position to share the same bedroom. Probably not. About some things, Jenny was still very naïve.

"I've ordered you a bath," she said when he entered. She had her jacket off and had laid out a day dress to change into.

"I know. I passed the maid on the stairs. Thank you."

"I'm sorry about what I said, Richard. Of course I am grateful to you for all that you've done for me. It's just that I seem to be nothing but trouble for you. First you had to rescue me that night at the inn, then, when I could no longer remain in Bath, you gave me a home and a position, and then you married me to save me from further scandal. I can't keep letting you save me all the time. I have to save myself."

"What do you need saving from now, Jenny? Dawson is gone. You've been accepted by Society as my wife, so you need no longer worry about the taint of scandal. It would seem that my services as errant knight are no longer required." Mortimer couldn't keep the anger out of his voice. He was tired, his leg bothered him, he wanted nothing more than a warm bath and a long nap. He'd had no sleep the night before. Though confident he could best Dawson in their sword fight, he was too experienced a soldier not to be apprehensive the night before a battle, even when that battle was a duel with an arrogant young man. The last thing he wanted to do right now was argue with Jenny.

"Well, good. I don't want a knight. I don't want a protector."

Mortimer stilled. "What do you want?"

"I want a husband."

Was she saying what he hoped she was saying? Had she noticed, even though he'd tried to hide it, that he was now able to make love to her? That he was able to be her husband in fact as well as in name?

"Jenny. . ." He reached for her to pull her close, to lavish her with kisses, to introduce her to the passion he knew they could share.

The maid chose that moment to knock on the door. Without hesitation, Jenny called out for her to come in. Following the maid came a footman carrying buckets of steaming water. Two more carried the metal tub and they proceeded to set it before the fire. Within minutes, his bath was ready and everyone was gone. Including his wife.

He'd wanted her to stay. He had visions of them sharing the bath together, both of them wet and naked. His body responded to his erotic thoughts and as he undressed, he looked down at himself, hard and ready. All he needed was a willing wife.

Was she willing?

As Mortimer squeezed his large body into the small tub, knees protruding above the water line, he thought again about what she'd said. She wanted a husband. She had a husband.

Didn't she?

A sick thought sank Mortimer's spirits. What if Jenny didn't know that he'd been restored? What if she meant she wanted a real husband, someone other than he?

What if Jenny had decided that this marriage of convenience they'd started was no longer convenient for her? He had offered her an annulment before and she'd turned him down.

But that was before Dawson had been dealt with,

before she saw that her life did not have to be spent hiding from scandal. She could have her old life back. They could quietly annul their marriage for the reason he'd told her before, that because of his injuries, he could not give her a child. A marriage unconsummated was no marriage at all.

Only now it could be consummated. Did Jenny know that? And if she did, would she want to stay married to him? She wanted a husband, but did she want him to be her husband?

∞∞∞∞

Jenny changed quickly in the dressing room attached to their bedroom, then exited through the hallway door so as not to disturb Richard in his bath. She went downstairs to order breakfast but found that it was already being served. Her father was alone in the dining room. It was the first time they had been alone together since that awful afternoon in Bath. Though they'd been sharing a house for several days, they'd successfully avoided having a private conversation.

"Where is your husband this morning? Is he all right?" Douglas dismissed the servants with a wave and soon he and Jenny were completely alone. "Did he meet Dawson this morning?" he asked in a low, confidential tone. "Did they duel?"

"There was no duel," Jenny said defensively. "Duels are illegal. They did meet for a friendly fencing match. Richard won handily by the way. I believe Dawson was sufficiently mortified and has decided to do some traveling."

"Glad to be rid of him," Douglas muttered.

"Really, Father, when you were so eager to see me married to him?" Jenny didn't even try to disguise her bitterness. "At least my husband is willing to stand up for my honor."

"Jenny." That one word held warning, yet Jenny no longer needed to heed it. Her father was not the man she had promised to love, honor, and obey.

"I thought you loved me," she said quietly and all the pain and disappointment she'd felt the previous year came flooding forth. "I know I made a mistake, but you wanted to punish me for it for the rest of my life. I didn't go out on the terrace alone with Gerald Dawson so I could have relations with him, I went out to privately tell him I wasn't interested in him. That I didn't want him to court me anymore. I thought I could spare his feelings and save him embarrassment. I thought he was a gentleman and would behave as a gentleman should. That was the only mistake I made.

"But you. You chose to side with a man who had dishonored your own daughter. You chose to blame me rather than him. You chose to put me out on the street rather than admit that you made a mistake.

"You disappointed me, Father."

He didn't respond. She waited while he stared at his cooling breakfast plate and said nothing. No apology, no attempt to make amends. Jenny would have left then, defeated, had she not noticed the wetness of his eyes and watched as a tear coursed down his cheek.

Picking up his napkin, he wiped his face then stood abruptly.

"I did what I thought was best. For you, for your sister, for all of us. You should have told me what happened before Gerald Dawson came to me. You should have trusted me."

Jenny watched her father leave the dining room, and she realized she still loved him. She hated what he had done, disagreed with the decisions he'd made, but he was her father and she loved him with the unconditional love of a child.

But she was glad she no longer called his home her own. And she would make very sure that he did not repeat the mistakes he'd made with her with her sister.

Abigail and Delia joined her and a servant timidly poked his head in to see if it was all right to come in and serve them. Jenny nodded and the young man brought in fresh platters of meat and eggs from the kitchen.

Abigail looked disappointed to find Jenny alone.

"I thought that Mr. Carmody might come back with you after the duel."

Jenny glanced at the servant who kept his expression blank as all good servants were wont to do. She wasn't fooled by it, though. She knew he heeded every word that was said.

"There was no duel, only a friendly fencing match between two gentlemen. Your brother won, by the way."

"Oh, I knew that," Abigail said with the confidence of youth. "No one can best Richard with sword or pistol. He's a soldier after all."

"He was a soldier. Now he's a landed gentleman who occasionally fences for enjoyment." Jenny wanted to make sure that no rumors about a duel germinated from this house. She wanted no investigation into Gerald Dawson's coincidental disappearance the morning he dueled with Richard.

"Please pass the toast," Delia said politely. "I think it's terribly romantic to have a man fight a duel for you."

"There was no duel!" Jenny declared. If she couldn't quell the rumor within her own family, how was she to stamp it out among Society?

"What's this about a duel?" Richard entered the room fresh from his bath, his hair still damp, dressed casually in trousers and shirt with no jacket or cravat. He looked devilishly handsome and her heart beat faster at the sight of him.

"I was trying to explain to the girls that you merely had a friendly fencing match this morning with Gerald Dawson. That there was no duel." She gave him a warning look so that he dared not dispute her.

"A fencing match in which I trounced him handily, so handily in fact that in his embarrassment he decided to hie himself off to sea, a ready and time honored way for young men to repair their finances."

Richard walked behind her chair and gave her a peck on her cheek before taking the place her father had vacated at the head of the table. Her father's uneaten breakfast had been cleared and within minutes Richard ate heartily of his own.

It amazed Jenny that he could have such an appetite after all that had transpired that morning. She found herself unable to take more than a few bites.

"Was Mr. Carmody at the fencing match this morning?" Abigail asked before biting into a butter-lathered scone.

"He was. I invited him to join us for breakfast, but he declined." Seeing the disappointment on her face, he quickly added, "but I suspect he will call later in the day."

"He must be very busy in his surgery," Abigail readily excused him.

"When he does stop by, I hope he will give you permission to travel back to Fairleigh. I am ready to go home," Jenny said. Accepted by London Society or not, Jenny longed to return to Fairleigh where Richard's leg could heal and she could resume her life as the wife of a country gentleman. And try not to cause him any more trouble.

She called Fairleigh home. The thought warmed him. The worry that she wanted to leave him had stayed with him all through his bath and as he dressed. He needed to get her alone so they could talk. What had she meant by wanting a husband?

"Mrs. Mortimer," he said formally. "Would you care to take a drive in the park this morning?"

She looked at him in surprise.

"If that's what you'd like to do, I'll join you, but truthfully, Richard, I am quite tired and had thought to retire to our room right after breakfast."

That would do, too.

"A nap sounds delightful, madam, do you mind if I join you?" Anyone hearing their exchange would assume that, like any normal married couple, they were planning a daytime tryst. If he had his way, he'd see to it that they were.

Jenny excused herself and returned to their room. Mortimer quickly finished his meal and started after her. He was almost to the foot of the stairs when Mr. Carlisle waylaid him.

"A word, Mortimer," his father-in-law said from the study doorway.

Mortimer looked longingly up the stairs to where his wife awaited him. He wanted to refuse, put Carlisle off, tell him they'd talk some other time. But, he couldn't. They were guests in the man's house, he owed him his time. Reluctantly, Mortimer walked toward the study.

THIRTEEN

"Would you like a cup of tea, or something stronger?"

"I'm fine. Just had breakfast."

Douglas Carlisle poured himself a cup of tea from the pot that sat on a silver tray on his desk. The desk was solid mahogany, finely crafted. Everything in the room, and in the entire house for that matter, was the best quality, the finest money could buy.

"I'm a wealthy man," Douglas began as though reading Mortimer's thoughts. Mortimer nodded in agreement. "I had intended to dower both of my daughters when they married. You and Jenny married without my permission or my blessing."

"I don't want your money," Mortimer said.

"I wasn't planning on giving you any. However, Jenny made me see this morning how much I wronged her. I am giving Jenny a trust. I will administer it, but it will belong to her. If she ever finds herself in a situation where she is in need of funds, I want to make sure she has some available to her. Without asking your permission. Or mine, for that matter. The trust will be openly accessible to her."

"In case she decides to leave me, you mean."

"She married you to avoid marrying Dawson," Douglas said bluntly. "I want to give her a choice."

Mortimer wanted to say something about the choices he'd given Jenny the previous summer when she ran away from a forced marriage, but he restrained himself. He wanted Jenny to have a choice, too. If she didn't want to stay married to him, at least she could live independently and would not have to return to her father's house.

For once, he and Jenny's father were in agreement.

By the time he reached their room, he'd lost the opportunity to speak privately with Jenny. She was sound asleep and he hadn't the heart to wake her. Instead, he removed his boots and lay down on the bed beside her. As she tended to do, Jenny rolled into him and nestled in the crook of his arm. He pulled her close.

He loved the feel of her beside him. In sleep, she looked sweet and innocent. Completely trusting.

Would she see his renewed virility as a betrayal? Or, as he hoped, as an opportunity for them to move forward with their life together. Would she be willing to try making love with him? After losing Dawson's child, would she want to have one with him?

He couldn't think of anything he wanted more than to have a child with Jenny. She was refined and gentle, yet had enough strength of character to keep from being considered bland.

She could be a fierce ally as she'd demonstrated when he was healing from his surgery and this morning when she was willing to shoot Dawson herself should Dawson have caused him harm.

As he drifted off to sleep, he had a vision of Jenny and him at Fairleigh surrounded by their brood. He fell asleep with a smile lingering on his face.

Nelson woke him just before noon. Mortimer found

himself alone in the bed—Jenny had left without him even waking. When had he lost his soldier's instinct for self-preservation? In all the years he'd been a military man, he'd been a light sleeper and would never have allowed a woman to leave his bed unnoticed. He must be growing soft in civilian life.

"All's taken care of, Captain," Nelson reported. "Once I explained things to him, Dawson decided it would be best to volunteer. I took him to the naval office and he signed on as a seaman. I made sure he boarded the ship to which he was assigned and waited until it weighed anchor and set sail. Gerald Dawson is on his way to patrol the coast of France."

"Good." Mortimer donned his boots. "I hope he becomes a better man because of the experience. Now, have you seen my wife?"

"Passed her on the stairs as I was heading up to see you, sir. She wore her cloak and was on her way out with the other ladies. More shopping, I believe, sir."

∞∞∞∞

If he hadn't known better, he would have thought she was avoiding him. For two days, Mortimer was unable to get his wife alone for more than five minutes. Carmody invited the family to the theater the evening after the duel. In his note to Mortimer, he stipulated that it was important for Mortimer to be seen in public to dispel any rumors that might be circulating. Indeed, more than one gentleman made comments about fencing matches.

Dawson's disappearance went largely unremarked upon, which surprised Mortimer. Apparently, the man was universally disliked and had only been tolerated because of his family background. No one lamented the fact that he had decided to go to sea.

Jenny received Carmody's permission for them to travel to Fairleigh, so she spent the day following the duel in busy preparations. Letitia and Abigail were invited to remain in Town with the Carlisles, which was a happy circumstance given that Abigail and Delia had become inseparable. However, before the invitation was issued, Jenny was required to spend hours with first Abigail, then Delia, then her mother, and finally her father and Letitia in negotiating the agreement.

Finally, two days after he'd fought a duel for her, he found himself alone with his wife. They were in their carriage on the Bath road making their way home to Fairleigh.

"Are you sorry we are not staying for the Season?" he asked when they got underway. While returning to Fairleigh so soon had been Jenny's idea, he wanted to make sure she wasn't doing it because she thought it was what he wanted. It was what he wanted, but more than returning to Fairleigh, he wanted Jenny to be happy. She had seemed to be enjoying the entertainments and activities.

"Not at all. I am anxious to get home."

There it was again. She called Fairleigh home.

"Jenny, there is something I need to speak to you about," he began.

Jenny put her hand up to stop him.

"I know all about it, Richard." His heart leaped to his throat but dropped as she continued. "My father told me about the trust fund. As far as I am concerned, the funds are there for both our use. If you need to make improvements to Fairleigh, I would be happy to contribute."

"I assure you, madam wife, I do not require your financial assistance."

"Well, I don't understand why my father didn't give

you the money as my dowry. He was certainly planning on dowering me when he married me off to Dawson."

"Let us not talk about Gerald Dawson, shall we?" But how could they not speak of him? He was the reason Mortimer was afraid to tell his wife that he wanted to bed her. Gerald Dawson may be miles away at sea, but he may as well have been seated in the carriage between them.

"If it wasn't the dowry, what did you want to talk to me about?" Jenny asked.

Suddenly, a moving carriage did not seem to be the appropriate place to have the discussion he needed to have with her.

"It can wait until we get home." Mortimer hoped that nothing delayed their journey.

ooooo

He was a coward. They'd been home at Fairleigh for almost a week, and he still hadn't talked to Jenny. She'd returned to her own room, and he hadn't even asked her to come back to his bed to sleep with him.

With Letitia still in London, Jenny made Fairleigh her own. The servants responded to her soft voice and gentle ways as they had never done to his mother's sharp orders and autocratic pronouncements. He had to admit, the house ran more smoothly now than it ever had, at least in his memory.

He loved watching Jenny take charge, loved listening to her stories at the dinner table each night. They had settled into the perfect picture of domestic bliss.

With one glaring exception.

He became obsessed. He had only to see her for his male appendage to snap to attention. It was embarrassing. Frustrating.

He needed to figure out how to seduce his wife

without frightening her. Without losing her.

His leg had much improved. He spent the days walking the estate with Mr. Godfrey. The exercise had done wonders for him. He no longer needed the assistance of a cane or walking stick. He barely even limped anymore.

The time had come for him to try riding horseback.

∞∞∞∞

"Would you care to come riding with me this morning?" Richard asked Jenny over breakfast.

"Are you sure you are able?" She had noticed the improvement in his walking. He seemed much stronger. But was he ready to ride? She would hate to have to drag Carmody down from London—Abigail especially would want to thrash her.

"I believe it is time for me to find out."

Nelson helped him to mount. He chose a gelding, large but well-schooled. Jenny chose a calm, sweet-tempered mare. She wanted to make sure that nothing caused Richard's horse to become excited.

She needn't have worried. Richard sat comfortably in the saddle, an experienced horseman once again at home where he belonged. She could picture him astride a stallion leading his men in battle. His posture was straight, he held the reins loosely in his hand, and controlled the beast with his knees.

She was a competent rider herself. Her father had always kept a good stable. But she was not at the same level as Richard. He was magnificent.

She felt again the stirring low in her belly that seemed to plague her lately whenever she was around him. Like the way he had made her feel at the Ashfords' ball—all jittery and excited as if something was going to happen, she just didn't know what. Sometimes she would catch him looking at her with such longing in his eyes it frightened her while at the same time made her want to answer that longing with her own.

Seeing Richard astride the gelding, so obviously in his element, she realized he was no longer the near invalid he had been when they'd met. Fully restored to health and fitness, Richard no longer needed her to advocate for him. She would never wish him to suffer what he had endured before, but at least while ill or recovering from surgery, she was useful to him.

Now, what could he possibly need her for? Though she made herself useful by managing his house, she knew that Letitia could do it just as easily, had done it, in fact, for Richard's whole life. No, Richard didn't need her, had never needed her really.

But she needed him. Not as her defender and protector, but as her friend. Her partner. Her husband.

They rode through the meadow where the sheep grazed contentedly, rode between the fields planted with crops, rode up the Bath road a bit before turning back. Mortimer felt good, comfortable and confident in the saddle, but he didn't want to overdo his first time out.

Jenny was a competent horsewoman, he was pleased to see. He hadn't thought to ask before if she rode. He realized there were many things he didn't know about her. He liked to think he had an entire lifetime to find them out.

As they rode home along the Bath road, side by side on the country lane, Mortimer experienced a contentment he had never felt before in his entire life. As a child, he was ever on guard against his father's unpredictable temper and his mother's constant harping. As an officer, he held men's lives in his hands. While there were often many hours, days, weeks even, of utter boredom, they were contrasted by the moments of stark fear and utter horror. Contentment was never part of a soldier's vocabulary.

Coming home to Fairleigh had required adjustment. His life was no longer ordered by military precision. He had to learn about crops and agriculture and estate management. Overriding all had been the pain and the fear of losing his leg, or worse, his life because of it.

Through it all had been Jenny. Helping her had helped him. She had helped him.

He reached across to pat her arm, which was the only part of her that he could safely reach. Had they not been on horseback, he would have pulled her into his arms.

"Thank you, Jenny, for standing by me while I healed."

Jenny blushed. "I'm glad you are well, Richard."

It was not the ideal moment, but perhaps there was no ideal moment. He'd certainly not found one since Carmody had pronounced him fully recovered. She'd presented him with an opportunity, and he needed to muster up his courage to make use of it.

"I am well, Jenny. Completely well. In all ways. I am no longer unable to perform my marital duties."

There, he'd said it.

Jenny pulled hard on her reins and her mare, placid as she was, reared in protest.

"Jenny!" Mortimer yelled, reaching for the bridle to bring her horse back under control. Jenny kept her seat, but was obviously flustered, whether by the behavior of her horse or by his announcement, he could not tell.

"I'm sorry. I've been trying to think of a way to tell you."

"You want to. . ."

"I want to make love to you, Jenny. I want to father a child with you." Having finally opened the subject, he found it surprisingly easy to declare his desires. "Jenny, I love you. Will you be my wife? Will you let me love you with my body as well as with my heart?"

They had stopped their horses in the middle of the road. A farmer's wagon approached and they moved off to the side. Jenny seemed fascinated by the stone wall that ran along the side of the road. She wouldn't look at him.

"Jenny?"

"I don't know, Richard. I have to think. I don't know." With that, she kicked her horse into motion and cantered toward home.

Mortimer caught up to her but followed behind her mare. He didn't try to pursue the discussion.

∞∞∞

Jenny gave her mount to a groom to unsaddle and brush down. Normally, she would have insisted on doing it herself as any good horsewoman would. But this wasn't a normal day.

"Jenny," Richard said when he'd dismounted. He reached out his hand, but she avoided it. She ignored him and almost ran by him she was so anxious to get away. She had to be alone. She needed to think.

He let her go. She knew he could have stopped her, but he let her go. She raced out the stable doors and was nearly to the house before she turned back to look at him. He moved a little stiffly but seemed otherwise none the worse for their ride.

He was well, he'd told her.

Jenny ran to her room. Her maid was there changing the bedding.

"Would you like a bath, ma'am?" Nellie asked politely.

"Later. Please finish that later, Nellie." Jenny ushered the girl out of the room and latched the door behind her.

She rested her forehead on the door and stood there trying to collect herself.

Ever since Richard had made his pronouncement, she'd been tormented by one overriding emotion. Fear.

Was she afraid of Richard or afraid of herself?

She was afraid that this life she had made for herself, this life that Richard had given her, was over. Their marriage had been based on the understanding that it would never be consummated. When she'd lost the baby, Richard had assured her that it would be a marriage in name only. That he was incapable of it being anything more.

He'd lied to her.

Even as she thought it, she knew it wasn't true. He couldn't have known that Mr. Carmody's surgery would heal him completely. None of them knew if he would even survive the surgery. He almost hadn't. She remembered how terrified she'd been that he would die those first few days when the fever had him in its grip.

No, Richard hadn't lied to her.

Jenny paced over to the window that overlooked the front lawn. She watched Richard return to the house after grooming his horse. He walked with confidence, with barely a trace of his former limp. Her heart jumped to her throat, but she couldn't name the emotion. There was fear, yes, but something else.

She sat on the window seat and stared at her boots.

She loved Richard and wanted to be his wife. But, she didn't think she was capable of being his wife the way he wanted her to be.

She allowed her mind to imagine being with Richard the way she'd been with Gerald Dawson. Panic clawed at her and she forced the images away. Gulping air into her lungs, she slid off the window seat and landed on her knees as dizziness assailed her. She felt faint.

If the very thought of having relations with her husband made her feel this way, how could she ever expect to get through the actual experience? She loved Richard, in her heart she knew it, but she could not make love with him.

His leg had healed, but she was still crippled by what Dawson had done to her.

There was only one thing for her to do. She had to release Richard from his marriage to her. Just as he had offered to free her when she lost the baby because he was not able to give her another one, she needed to free him so he could marry a woman who could really be his wife. A woman who would come happily and willingly to his bed. A woman who wanted to bear his children.

A pang centered low in her belly, in her womb. She would love to have Richard's baby. If there were any way she could bear him a son without having to endure the physical act of procreation, she would do it eagerly.

But she knew what the act entailed and she hadn't the courage to face it. Not even with Richard.

She could hear him moving about his room, changing out of his riding clothes. She went to the connecting door between their rooms and placed her hand on it, as though touching the door could touch him. She knew she should knock, should talk to him. She needed to tell him that while her heart wanted to make love, her mind and body would not allow it.

She needed to tell him that while he may be healed, she was not.

But she didn't knock. She kept her palm pressed flat against the door while a single tear ran down her cheek.

∞∞∞

Mortimer disgusted himself. He couldn't have handled

the situation with less finesse if he had tried. For days he had been trying to find the right moment, the gentlest words, to tell Jenny he wanted them to share all that marriage offered. Instead, he'd blurted it out in the middle of a road. Clumsily. Unthinkingly.

He removed his boot and threw it across the floor. It hit the connecting door between their rooms with a satisfying thud. Removing the second boot, he tossed it so that it followed the first, banging the door then landing on the floor.

The door sprang open and Jenny stood in the doorway looking like a frightened deer eyeing the barrel of a shotgun. He was on his feet and closing the distance between them before she had a chance to bolt. Without saying a word, he grabbed her hand and pulled her into the room, closing the door behind her.

She looked like she expected him to ravish her. He pulled her into his arms and stroked her back, resting her head on his shoulder, trying to gentle her the way he would a skittish colt.

"Jenny, Jenny, I'm so sorry. I had planned a gentle wooing, not a thoughtless blurting."

"It's all right," she mumbled into his chest. "I needed to know. Now we can decide what to do."

Mortimer's hand stilled at the small of her back. "We don't have to do anything, Jenny, not until you are ready."

Jenny pulled away from him, putting some distance between them.

"I won't ever be ready, Richard. I'm sorry, but I can't give you what you want. All I can offer you is your freedom so that you can find a woman who will." Her voice choked on the last sentence.

"Jenny, I don't want any other woman but you. I love you."

Jenny's tears flowed then and she threw herself into

Mortimer's arms. "I love you, too, Richard. And I can't. . .if I can't even think about. . ."

"What, Jenny? What are you trying to say?"

She looked at him then, and his heart ached for all the pain and anguish he saw in her eyes.

"If not you, then who? If I could with anyone it would be you. And I can't. Not even for you. I can't." She said the last with more determination. It was like she was pronouncing a life sentence.

FOURTEEN

Mortimer brought Jenny to the seating area in front of the fireplace. It was cold, unlike the night she'd stood in front of it and agreed to wed him. He eased her into one of the cushioned seats and knelt on one knee in front of her.

"I have bungled this badly," he admitted. "Nothing has to change between us if you don't want it too. But after the duel you said you wanted a husband. I was afraid that you meant you wanted to marry a man who could be a real husband to you, including in the bedroom. I needed you to know that if that's what you want, you can have it with me. But I would never force myself on you. You have to believe me on that. You have to trust me."

Jenny looked into his eyes, which were even with hers, and saw the truth there.

"I know you would never hurt me, Richard." She stroked the side of his face with her hand. "That's why this is so difficult. I know you would sacrifice your life for me. I can't let you. You need a wife who can give you sons. Now that you are able to be a father, you need a woman who can become mother to your children. I know how much you want children, Richard. You were willing to raise Gerald Dawson's child as your own."

"I won't lie to you. I want children. And I want you to be their mother."

"And I'm telling you that I can't be." She said it with finality.

Mortimer sat back on his heel. They had reached an impasse. He needed a new strategy, fast.

"Give me six months to woo you, Jenny. If I can't convince you that making love with me will be nothing like what Dawson did to you, then we will annul the marriage. You can go live quietly somewhere in the country, if that's what you want. I will support you."

"You won't have to, I have the money my father put aside for me."

"I will support you," he said firmly. "All I ask is that you allow me to woo you. You can feel passion, Jenny, I know you can. When I kiss you, when you snuggle up beside me at night, when I hold you in my arms, I know you aren't afraid. You respond to me, Jenny."

"Kisses and hugs are not all you are asking for."

"No, I admit, I want more. But kisses and hugs are a good place to start. Sharing a bed at night like we used to is also a good beginning. Let me woo you, Jenny. Let me show you what it's like to have a husband."

She didn't want to leave him, would use any excuse to stay. It was foolish, she knew. Six months wouldn't change anything, would only make it harder to leave. But if she couldn't give him what he wanted, she could at least give him this.

Once he realized that time would make no difference, be it six months, a year, or ten years, he would be anxious to see her go.

"Six months," she agreed. She would use it to store up the memories she would need to cherish for the rest of her life.

∞∞∞∞

Mortimer began his campaign with subtle maneuvers rather than frontal assaults. He'd asked for six months but had no intention of allowing it to go on for that long. If he couldn't seduce his wife in just a few weeks, he would admit defeat. He had no intention of losing.

He was not a man inexperienced in the art of lovemaking. He had always been selective in his liaisons, not poking every piece that offered itself like many of the men he soldiered with. There were always women following the battalion, willing women selling their services to lonely men far away from home. While Mortimer had availed himself of a prostitute a time or two, he preferred to engage with women who meant something to him.

He had had a six-month liaison with a widow in Portugal. Marie was sensuous and seductive and had enjoyed a healthy relationship with her late husband. She knew what she wanted, a man to share her bed but who would not intrude upon her life. From Marie, he'd learned how to please a woman and how to engage in sexual activity for the pleasure of both partners.

Their affair ended when Marie decided to accept a marriage offer from a very wealthy older man who could offer her the security and protection a foreign-born soldier could not. Mortimer had helped her grieve her late husband, had allowed her to enjoy passion until she was ready to give herself in marriage to another man. Their parting had been friendly and mutual.

After Marie, he'd had a series of short-term affairs with various women, some for pay, others simply for mutual pleasure. He'd always tried, even with the women he hired, to give as good as he got. They always pretended to be satisfied at least.

He knew he was at worst a competent lover. He needed to call on all of his talent and skill to convince his wife to let him be her lover.

∞∞∞∞

Jenny reluctantly joined Richard in his bed that night. Nervously, she slipped under the covers beside him. He drew her close to his side as he had done before, but instead of relaxing against him and finding comfort as she always had, she lay stiff and afraid. It had been so easy to trust him when she knew he was unable to physically assault her. Lying with him had been like sharing a bed with a trusted friend. For years, she and Delia had slept together and being with Richard had had that familiar comfort, talking into the darkness, sharing secrets. She'd felt safe with him.

She didn't feel safe tonight. Even though he wore a nightshirt as he always did, she was aware of that male part of him that she had been able to ignore before. She didn't know what she expected from him, thought that he would touch her in places she didn't want to be touched, but he did nothing. He simply pulled her close and before she knew it, he was snoring softly beside her.

He didn't try to ravish her. He didn't make any demands on her. He fell asleep.

Jenny relaxed and turned on her side, snuggling up next to Richard's sleeping form. She let her arm drape across his stomach as she had grown accustomed to doing and fell soundly asleep. Her last waking thought was how much she had missed this closeness and how much better she slept in Richard's bed.

He kissed her awake the next morning. She felt his

warm lips on her eyelids then moving to her cheek, finally resting on her lips. What a wonderful sensation. She pretended to be asleep so he would continue kissing her. She liked it when Richard kissed her. He stroked his tongue along her lips and she opened her mouth in response. She could no longer pretend sleep when his tongue plunged into her mouth. That felt too strange, almost frightening, and she pulled back from it.

He stopped as soon as he felt her resistance.

"Good morning," he said. And when she opened her eyes, he smiled down at her. For a moment she felt trapped, but then she realized he lay on his side and wasn't bearing down on top of her in any way.

"Good morning," she managed to answer.

"I've missed sleeping with you. It feels so good to have you back in my bed." And that was that. Richard got up and donned his robe. It was the same as it had been before his recovery.

Jenny wasn't sure why she felt disappointed.

"I thought we would go into Bath today and visit your Aunt Julia."

His pronouncement surprised Jenny. She had expected Richard to spend all of his time trying to seduce her. Visiting Julia would not present him with many opportunities to do so. Visibly relaxing, she smiled and agreed to the trip.

∞∞∞∞

They stopped at the Carsons' cottage along the way. Jenny had sent them a note and some gifts months ago, but this was the first time they had been able to stop by in person. The Carsons were pleased to see Richard walking so well.

Seeing the cottage in summer with flowers blooming

in the front garden made that awful, icy winter day when they'd had the carriage accident seem like nothing more than a bad dream.

"I'm so pleased to see that Captain Mortimer has recovered from his injuries," Mrs. Carson said as she and Jenny walked ahead of the men on a tour of the garden.

"Mr. Carmody is a fine surgeon and saved not only his leg, but his life, I believe."

"And have you recovered from your misfortune?" Mrs. Carson asked gently.

Jenny answered very carefully. "I was almost consumed by sorrow, but now I believe I am whole again."

"Losing a babe is something you never fully recover from," Mrs. Carson said sagely. "But having another child eases the sorrow somewhat."

Jenny looked down, a blush pinkening her cheeks.

There was something about Mrs. Carson's motherly ways that drew out confidences. Without realizing she was going to do it, Jenny found herself opening to the older woman.

"There won't be any children. Captain Mortimer would like to try, but I am afraid."

"Are you afraid of having another miscarriage? Surely it was the accident that caused you to lose your baby, Mrs. Mortimer. There's no reason to suspect you won't carry the next one to term."

"It isn't having a baby that I am afraid of," Jenny admitted, "but the very act of conception."

"Was the captain not gentle with you? I'll have Mr. Carson speak to him for you if that's the case."

Jenny's cheeks felt blood red now, she was so embarrassed. She could not imagine having such a conversation with her own mother. But Mrs. Carson was a midwife, she did not shy away from such topics.

"Before his surgery, Captain Mortimer was not able to. . .that is, he thought he never would. . .it wasn't Captain Mortimer who was ungentle," Jenny finished lamely. She was relieved that Mrs. Carson seemed to understand because she was sure she could not have explained it any better.

"This other man, he fathered the baby you lost?"

Jenny nodded.

"And did you love him the way you love Captain Mortimer?"

Jenny looked at Mrs. Carson aghast. "Certainly not. He was a brutal, vicious man who forced himself on me."

"Then you have no reason to deny Captain Mortimer his rights as your husband. I don't believe you have any cause for concern, Mrs. Mortimer. Anyone can see how much the captain cares for you. Do you really believe he will behave the same way that other man did?"

"Of course not, but Mrs. Carson, how do I keep that other man out of my thoughts? How do I lose this unreasoning fear?"

"By keeping your eyes open and your thoughts on Captain Mortimer." Mrs. Carson patted Jenny's hand. "And think how wonderful it will be to have a baby with the man you love."

∞∞∞∞

Julia was thrilled to see them and invited them to stay for several days. Mortimer was relieved at the invitation. Spending one night with Jenny in his bed and keeping his hands off her had taken all his strength of will. He felt more confident of his ability not to ravish his wife if they were sleeping under her aunt's roof than his own. He needed to gentle Jenny like he would a fractious pony. Get her used to his hand before attempting to ride her.

They spent the days in Bath taking the waters. Though healed, his leg still experienced an occasional stiffness that the mineral waters of Bath seemed to help.

Jenny relaxed around him, knowing he would not press her in her aunt's house. It gave him an opportunity to woo her gently, a caress here, a touch there. He kissed her palm and watched her eyes widen in surprise at the warmth that spread through her.

She was not immune to him, he knew. He caught her watching him when she didn't think he was looking. He recognized that look in her eyes. It was a very womanly look, a very heated look. She may think she was incapable of consummating her marriage with him, but he knew that with a little coaxing, he could have her writhing with passion beneath him.

∞∞∞∞

It was now or never. They'd arrived home that afternoon. The trip to Bath had allowed them to be together without any of the responsibilities that came with running the estate. It had enabled them to enjoy each other's company without the constant crises that had plagued them in the early days of their marriage.

In Bath, Mortimer had courted Jenny as he would have if her father hadn't sent her running to Fairleigh for his help.

He knew that Jenny trusted him. Tonight, he would put that trust to the test.

∞∞∞∞

Jenny's maid, Nellie, tested the water in the bath she'd prepared.

"Would you like me to stay and help you with your bath, Mrs. Mortimer?"

"No, thank you, Nellie, you run along. I'll be fine."

Alone in her bedchamber, Jenny disrobed behind the screen that blocked the bathtub from the rest of the room. Though summer, Nellie had lit a small fire in the grate to keep the bath water warm and Jenny sank into the tub soothed by its warm comfort. She heard a door open and close and assumed it was Nellie leaving the room.

She was wrong.

"May I be of assistance, Mrs. Mortimer?"

Richard spoke from the other side of the screen. Jenny felt a moment of panic, then forced herself to relax.

"No, thank you, Richard." She trusted him to give her her privacy. Part of her wanted to leap from the tub and hide her nakedness in her robe, horrified by the thought that only the flimsy wooden screen separated him from her.

Another part of her, a part she didn't recognize, felt a fluttering of excitement knowing he stood mere inches away. That part wanted him to peek around the screen to examine her naked body.

"I asked for our dinner to be sent to my room," he said, and she could practically feel his breath on her neck even though she knew he was still safely on the other side of the screen. "Will you join me when you are done?"

Jenny was about to say yes and send him away when Mrs. Carson's advice came back to her. This was Richard, not some stranger who wanted to humiliate her. This was her husband, the man she loved.

"Richard," Jenny said before she had a chance to change her mind, before rational thought and unreasoning fears stopped her. "Perhaps you could wash my back for me."

Mortimer wasn't sure he'd heard her correctly, but he wasn't willing to chance questioning her invitation. He was around the screen before she had an opportunity to retract it. He stayed behind her, allowing her to hide or reveal what she wanted to him. It was warm behind the screen with the steam from the bath water and the low fire burning. Mortimer rolled up his sleeves and knelt behind the tub. Picking up a sponge, he allowed it to caress her back and neck. Jenny leaned forward, allowing him access. Though he could feel her spine go rigid, she didn't pull away from his touch.

He followed the sponge with his lips, kissing her neck and back.

She shuddered.

"Jenny," he murmured.

"Please don't say anything, Richard, just take me before my courage fails."

He smiled. She offered herself like a sacrificial victim. Unable to resist the sensual pull, yet still expecting pain and humiliation.

He would have to remedy that.

"I'm not going to take you, Jenny," he said, running the sponge down her arm, letting warm, soapy water spill over her.

"You're not?" She turned her head to peek at him, the relief unmistakable in her voice.

He smiled. "No. You are going to take me."

She turned away and huddled in the water as though she were chilled. Mortimer stood and retrieved a towel. Coming around the side of the tub, he held it open for her.

"I'll avert my eyes if you want me to," he offered.

She shook her head and bravely forced herself to stand, exposing her nakedness to him. Mortimer swallowed at the sight. His wife was beautiful. He didn't allow his eyes to feast on her the way he wanted but kept them trained on her face so she would not become too anxious.

Jenny stepped out of the tub into his waiting arms. He wrapped the towel around her, careful to release his hold as soon as it was done so she would not feel constrained in any way. He had learned Jenny enjoyed being held, but not when he held her too tightly or she felt she couldn't get free.

He picked up her robe while she dried herself off and held it for her as she slipped her arms into its sleeves. He trailed his lips along her neck and felt her shudder.

Jenny turned and lifted her lips to him for a kiss.

"I had a talk with Mrs. Carson when we visited on our way to Bath," she said when the kiss ended. "She convinced me that I should try."

"Jenny," Mortimer breathed the word then kissed her again. He ran his tongue along her lips and Jenny opened her mouth, allowing him entrance. He kissed her deeply, exploring her mouth with his tongue. She stiffened and he could feel her fighting not to pull away. Abruptly, he ended the kiss, but Jenny was determined. She pulled him to her again and this time, her tongue joined his in a heated dance.

Mortimer held himself in check, though he wanted to lift her in his arms and carry her to his bed. Instead, he broke the kiss, which left them both panting, and gave her his arm.

"Shall we adjourn to the other room and have our dinner?"

"Should I dress?"

Mortimer smiled. "You are dressed perfectly for what I have in mind," he assured her.

∞∞∞∞∞

They sat on the sofa in the seating area, as far from the

bed as the room would allow. Nervous, Jenny had little appetite, but Richard insisted on feeding her. He picked up an olive and put it in her mouth, allowing her to taste his fingers as he did so, which for some reason made her feel a slight tug low in her belly.

"Remember the first night we met, when I fed you a bite of meat pie?" he asked.

She nodded and he placed a piece of cheese between her lips. There was something sensual about the way he fed her, something carnal. Jenny picked up an olive and put it in his mouth. He tugged on her fingertips and it made her gasp. Grasping her hand, Richard kissed her palm then trailed kisses up her arm, letting the belled sleeve of her robe slide up to her elbow. His grip was loose—she knew she could pull away if she wanted. She didn't want to.

Richard's thigh brushed her knee, and she reached down to rest her hand on it. It was hard and solid beneath her palm. She was aware of him as a man in a way she had never been before. As he kissed her neck, her eye drifted down and she saw the bulge in his trousers that showed his arousal.

Jenny froze.

FOURTEEN

Mortimer felt the change in her immediately. One moment she was responding to him and the next she grew still. Her breath quickened, but not with passion. With fear.

"Jenny," he said softly. She met his eyes and he wanted to cry with sadness and frustration. Her eyes were tortured, wild with panic. Like a deer seeing a hunter, whose one thought was of escape.

Slowly, calmly, he moved away from her. He got up from the sofa and stood in front of the fireplace with one hand resting on the mantel, head bowed.

"I'm sorry," Jenny whispered.

Mortimer turned and faced her. She looked so dejected sitting there alone. Dejected yet relieved.

He started unbuttoning his shirt.

"What are you doing?" He detected the note of panic in her voice, but he continued.

"I am undressing," he said calmly, reasonably. "I want you to see my body, Jenny, all of it, so that perhaps you won't fear it."

Jenny swallowed, but nodded her assent. Mortimer

removed his shirt and Jenny gasped.

"Oh, Richard!" He knew what she was seeing. His chest was scarred from old wounds, a French bayonet had nicked him below his right rib and he had a burn on his left breast. A man did not survive ten years in the military unscathed.

Jenny wanted to run her hands on his chest, to kiss the scars he carried there. But she remained seated because Richard had kicked off his shoes and removed his hose. Now he pulled down his breaches, leaving him only in his small clothes. Jenny blinked. She expected him to stop, but he took off his small clothes and stood before her completely exposed. Naked.

Richard stood erect and very still, knowing that any move he made might frighten her. Jenny couldn't help herself, she let her eyes roam over him, from the top of his head to the tips of his toes. His chest was not the only part of his body that carried scars. There was the white, puckered scar on his thigh, of course, but other marks marred his skin.

His legs she had seen before, when she'd nursed him after his surgery. She'd watched Mr. Carmody change his bandaging. She was not surprised by the light sprinkling of dark hair. His chest, also, sported a dusting of dark hair that trailed down to his navel. She examined his bare arms and torso but kept darting away from looking at his groin.

Her face flamed red and she wanted to look away, but he wouldn't let her.

"Look at me, Jenny," he said in his officer's voice and she obeyed. She looked at him, at that part of him that caused her to want to shy away. It stood erect, long and hard, pointing at the ceiling. Two soft sacs, covered in hair, hung loosely beneath it.

She had never before seen the naked male form. She

had felt Dawson's hardness but had never seen it. She had conjured an image of it that was far worse than the reality. Standing before her stark naked, Richard did not look frightening at all. In fact, he looked rather silly.

Jenny smiled and Mortimer relaxed. She wasn't running screaming from the room. She giggled.

He looked down at himself. He was hard with wanting. He'd elicited many reactions from women in the past, but humor was not one of them. Jenny looked so relieved, however, that he couldn't get angry with her or be insulted. He did the only thing he could do. He laughed with her.

"I didn't think I looked that amusing," he said.

"You have no idea what I expected." Tears formed at the corners of her eyes, but they weren't tears of fright. They were tears of laughter.

"Come here, Jenny," he said. It wasn't an order, but a request. Jenny stood in front of him and placed her hand lightly upon his chest. He closed his eyes at her touch.

"Explore all you want, love. Touch everything." And she did. Tentatively at first, then more boldly. She ran her hands over his naked body. Mortimer stayed perfectly still allowing her freedom in her exploration. Her first soft touch on his shaft had him gasping, but he did not grab her hand and show her how to stroke him the way he wanted her to. She giggled when it jumped at her touch and he smiled.

She was such an innocent. She looked up into his eyes and said, "I'd like to try again."

He sat on the sofa and motioned for her to sit astride him. Her robe gaped in front but still kept her modestly covered.

"I would like to touch you now, Jenny," he said. "Just the way you explored me, I'd like to explore you. But you are in control. Take my hand and help me know your body.”

Nervous but willing, Jenny took his hand in hers and placed his palm on her stomach, then up to rest on her left breast. He didn't squeeze it the way he longed to but kept his hand relaxed and open, moving wherever she guided him. At first, she kept him carefully outside the robe so he felt only cloth, not skin. But as she got bolder, she allowed him to touch the flesh of her chest where the robe gaped open. She brought his hand up to her face and rubbed it against her cheek, placing a soft kiss in the middle of his palm.

"Tell me what to do now, Richard."

"Untie your robe, Jenny. Let me see all of you."

Leaving his palm at her cheek, she untied the belt and allowed the robe to fall off her shoulders and pool at her waist.

Richard leaned forward and kissed her breasts, suckling gently on first one nipple then the next. He didn't touch her with his hands, letting his arms rest at his sides. Jenny sat very still for a moment, then leaned into him, giving him better access.

Warmth spread through her and she closed her eyes briefly, but as soon as she did, she wanted to pull away. Opening her eyes, she gazed down on Richard's head and watched him minister to her breasts and the wonderful sensation returned. This was Richard, not some stranger. This was her husband, the man she loved. And what he was doing to her made her feel warm and tingly and alive with anticipation. Her breathing grew rapid, and she felt the sensation building in the very core of her.

Richard leaned back and smiled up at her.

"May I touch you, Jenny?"

She nodded.

He pushed the robe off her lap and onto the floor then touched her intimately. Jenny almost leaped off of him but forced herself to remain. His touch was gentle, not painful. It was embarrassing, but also pleasant. He rubbed her, and the sensation that had ebbed started to build again.

"Jenny, lift yourself up and come down on top of me. Put me inside you. Let me love you," he said it urgently, pleadingly. She could not refuse him.

Awkwardly, she maneuvered herself so that her opening touched the tip of his erection. Richard guided himself into her, and she settled herself on him, taking him in a little bit at a time until he filled her. She lost her breath with the pleasure of it. She felt whole, fulfilled. Resting her hands on his shoulders, she leaned her head against his forehead and let herself experience a moment of profound relief. This marital act she shared with Richard bore no resemblance to the violence Dawson perpetrated upon her. This was an act of love. She wanted to stay perfectly still, connected to her husband in this intimate way, and never move.

But the sensation started to build again and she needed more.

"Ride me, Jenny," Richard said in a strangled whisper. Sweat beaded on his forehead.

She rose up, then settled back down again, slowly at first, but then found her rhythm.

Riding him hard and fast, she kept her eyes locked on his face and watched the play of pleasure on his features. Richard's hands rested lightly on her hips, but he didn't force her, he received her.

The pressure built and built until she felt an explosion of warmth and pleasure wash over her. She cried out and Richard shouted his release and she collapsed against him.

Jenny laughed, a joyful, remarkable sound she barely recognized as her own.

Richard stroked her back and she relaxed against him.

She sighed.

"Thank you, Richard. That was. . ." She lifted her head from where it rested on his chest and looked him in the eye. "That was like nothing I've ever experienced before."

Richard stroked her hair and face with his hand. "I knew it would be."

He eased her off of him and retrieved her robe from where it had fallen on the floor. After helping her into it, he returned to her room to get a cloth from the bath with which they cleaned themselves. He donned his dressing gown and they settled down to enjoy their dinner, a cold collation of meats, fruits, and cheese.

While they ate, they talked. Jenny talked again of the night Gerald Dawson had raped her, finally able to separate the violence of that experience from the passion she'd just shared with Richard.

"You may need to go slowly for awhile, Jenny, and fight the fear every time we make love, but I will do whatever I can to make it easier for you."

"Knowing that it is you, Richard, makes it easier for me. I love you."

They moved to the bed, sliding naked between the linen sheets. Jenny nestled in Richard's arms, tucked snugly under his shoulder, head leaning on his chest, and felt safe and content. She allowed her hand to wander down to that part of him she had feared and now accepted as him, Richard, the man she loved. She felt its softness and how it grew bigger and harder as she stroked. It made her feel powerful to have such control over him. Without him prompting, she climbed on top of him again and tried to insert him inside her, wanting to feel that wonderful sensation again.

"You're not ready, Jenny, and neither am I," Richard said softly even as he stroked her with his hand and made her ready for him. And when her body wept to receive him, he found that he was ready, too.

They made love for the second time in their married life. As Mortimer reached his release, he vowed to send Mrs. Carson a thank you gift for giving him his wife.

EPILOGUE

Fairleigh was bursting with people, both family and guests. Jenny brought Caroline up to the nursery so she could settle young Cameron in with his nurse.

"I am so glad you could come for the christening, Caroline," Jenny said, carrying her own son in her arms. Jordan Elliot Mortimer would be christened early the next morning in the village church with a celebration following at Fairleigh.

"I missed your wedding, I wasn't going to miss this," Caroline said. "Besides, I am the godmother after all."

Jenny gently placed Jordan, soundly asleep, into his bassinet without waking him. He was three weeks old and she still marveled at him, his perfectly shaped fingers and toes, his ears, and blue eyes that looked at her with such wisdom. He had a full head of chestnut hair, the same shade as Richard's.

He was a miracle, their son.

"We had asked Abigail and Mr. Carmody to be godparents, but they decided to run off to Gretna Green to get married. I hope you don't mind being second choice." Caroline was Jenny's closest friend. Jenny knew she wouldn't mind, had in fact offered to fill the vacancy when Jenny discovered the note from Abigail the previous morning. "I don't know why they felt they had to run off," Jenny sighed. "We would have given them a lovely wedding."

Caroline gave Jenny a knowing smile. "That's probably why."

Caroline had also married abruptly at the height of her first Season.

"Now I'll have to wait for Delia to wed for that big wedding celebration. You, me, now Abigail all married hastily."

"I'm glad to know that 'marry in haste, regret in leisure' is not a truism in our lives," Caroline said, watching Cameron crawl across the nursery to retrieve a toy. "Besides, we all married for love."

Jenny looked sharply at her friend and realized she'd never told her that she had married for convenience, not love. It didn't matter now. She was in love with her husband.

As if thinking of him conjured him, Richard appeared in the nursery doorway. He looked younger now that he'd shaved off his mustache.

"Sorry to bother you, my dear, but Letitia requires your presence in the kitchen."

Jenny shook her head. She and Letitia had spent the past year battling over who ran the house. It had become something of a game. Jenny gave an order and Letitia countermanded it. When Jenny quietly instructed the servants to do what she wanted done in the first place, Letitia fumed. Though Letitia avoided outright confrontation, she waged a stealth campaign worthy of a master.

"Now that Abigail is married," Jenny suggested hopefully, "do you think Letitia would be happier living with them?"

Richard laughed and kissed her quickly on her mouth.

Caroline beamed at him. "You've made her very happy," she said. "Thank you."

Richard bowed. "It has been my pleasure." He walked over and looked at his son sleeping so peacefully. A look of utter contentment came over his face.

No longer the hardened soldier he'd been when they'd first met, Jenny saw no sign of the strain that had marred his features when his leg injury pained him. Now, Richard was a country gentleman very much at home. She sighed.

Caroline rolled her eyes and scooped up Cameron.

"I think I'll keep him with me for a while longer," she said.

"And I'd better go deal with Letitia," Jenny said.

They left Richard alone with his son.

∞∞∞∞

Jenny left the house early the next morning, before getting Jordan ready for his trip to the church. She walked across the softening lawn, starting to thaw in the early March air. She entered the family cemetery and stopped at the stone Richard had set in place. Baby Mortimer.

Carrying Jordan had been a joy and a sorrow for her because she remembered this first baby. She didn't allow herself to love Jordan too much while he was in her womb, felt guilty at how much she had hated his brother when she carried him.

There was always the fear that she didn't deserve to be a mother because of the way she'd felt about her first child. She kept expecting God to take Jordan from her, too, especially if she loved him too much.

But now, Jordan was here and she had no choice but to love him. Her heart melted at her very first sight of him. When he cried the first time, filling his lungs with air and life, she'd cried with him.

But this child would always be her first. This child, conceived in anger and violence, had given her the life she now had. She knelt and cleared some dirt off the marker.

"I would have loved you," she said as she had so many times before. But for the first time, she realized it was a lie. Because she did love this child, this son who had died. And peace settled in her heart.

∞∞∞∞

Jordan Elliot Mortimer did not appreciate having cold water poured on his head. He put up quite a fuss as first Caroline, his godmother, then Nelson, his godfather, tried to comfort him. As soon as the ceremony was over, young Master Jordan was gratefully returned to the waiting arms of his parents. Richard quieted him in moments and soon had the babe sleeping in his arms.

The party returned to Fairleigh for breakfast. The conversation was lively around the table until Caroline said, "Jenny, did you hear the news about Gerald Dawson?"

Everyone grew quiet. Jenny shook her head.

"His name was on the list of seamen who drowned off the coast of Gibraltar last month. I thought for sure it must be some other Gerald Dawson, I couldn't imagine what a man of his stature would be doing as a common seaman aboard a warship, but my husband assured me it was the same man. He was notified by Dawson's solicitor, you see, because Mr. Dawson owed him a debt."

Thomas Perry nodded confirmation of his wife's statement.

Richard, who was sitting next to Jenny at the table,

placed his hand over hers. Tears sprang to Jenny's eyes and she looked at Richard, stricken. "Why am I crying?" she asked, as if he should know.

"Please excuse us," Richard said and escorted Jenny from the room.

Alone in their bedroom, Jenny turned into Richard's arms.

"I feel so foolish. Why am I crying for a man I despised?"

"Maybe it's relief, knowing that he is no longer in this world. Maybe it's sorrow for the man you thought him to be. It doesn't matter, Jenny. Just let yourself cry."

It was as if all the pain that Gerald Dawson had caused her was fresh and new. Jenny sobbed and railed, not sure what emotions were goading her—sorrow, anger, loss. So much loss. Her lost virginity, her lost innocence, her lost child. All of it rose to the surface and burst forth.

Richard held her, tightly when he feared she might hurt herself, loosely when she was finally spent.

A timid knock sounded on the door. Richard opened it to find Caroline standing outside.

"Jenny, I am so sorry, I didn't mean to upset you. It was just a piece of news. I had no idea Gerald Dawson had meant so much to you after you left him at the altar. It was unthinkingly foolish of me. Of course he meant something to you, you never would have agreed to marry him had he not. Please forgive me."

Caroline was Jenny's closest friend, yet she hadn't told her what Dawson had done, had never told her why she ran away from her wedding. She would have if she had needed to find refuge at Caroline's house in Cornwall, but when Richard took her in, she hadn't bothered. She'd allowed Caroline to believe what everyone else believed. That Richard was the reason she'd run away from Dawson. That she was running not from Dawson, but to

Richard, returned home from the war.

"I owe you an apology, Caroline," Jenny said. "I haven't told you the truth."

Richard politely left them alone and returned to their guests. Jenny sat Caroline down and told her everything, about Dawson, about her father disowning her, and how Richard had saved her. She even confessed about the duel and explained how Gerald Dawson had come to be on that warship that went down at sea.

Caroline was in tears by the time she finished. She'd started crying in earnest when Jenny told her about the baby she'd lost.

"Poor, poor Jenny. You must have felt so alone."

"I was never alone, thanks to Richard," Jenny said.

∞∞∞∞

Richard was in the nursery watching Jordan sleep. Jenny had made sure their guests were all sufficiently entertained in the drawing room before seeking him out.

"He's beautiful, isn't he?" she said when she came up beside him.

"Men don't like to be called beautiful," he said.

"He isn't a man yet. Just a baby. And he is beautiful."

"You are a stubborn woman." He said it without any bite. "I have been thinking about Gerald Dawson. Would it have been better if I had killed him on the dueling field? If I had thought it would free you from him, I would have."

"No. You did the right thing. I would not have that on your hands."

"I as much as killed him, though, didn't I?"

"You gave him a chance to start a new life. More than he deserved."

"I can't help feeling glad he's dead, though," Richard

admitted.

"I can't hate him anymore," Jenny said. "I hate what he did to me, but it brought me to you. I've been carrying this awful burden of hate inside and now it's gone. And I feel free."

Richard pulled Jenny into his arms. Together they watched their son sleep.

"I love you, Mrs. Mortimer," Richard said.

"And I love you, Captain Mortimer."

ABOUT THE AUTHOR

Terri Kennedy lives and writes on Cape Cod in a cottage by the sea that she and her husband share with a black lab mix who's afraid of the water and a cat who thinks he's a dog. After a career in high tech, she became a librarian where she could indulge her love affair with books. A martial artist, Terri at various times practiced tae kwan do, kensho ryu, and aikido and is currently studying tai chi. Please contact her through her web site www.terrikennedy.com.